DINOSAUR EMPIRE

"Now, what's this great mystery you want to show me?" Aaron asked.

Peter pointed at the Sphinx. "You're looking at it," he said.

Aaron frowned. For a moment he didn't get it. At first it looked just like the Sphinx. No, Aaron suddenly realized, it was more than that. It didn't have the familiar Sphinx face. Its face was weird . . . reptilian. "Oh my God," Aaron said suddenly, quietly.

"Recognize it?" Jennifer murmured.

"Do I? It's Klaido." Klaido was a Gairk, a cousin of the Mutata. Klaido wasn't kindly disposed to the humans. He had, in fact, vowed to kill them all on sight. "What does this mean?" Aaron asked after a long moment.

"I don't know," Jennifer said.

"But I doubt it's anything good," added Peter.

ALSO AVAILABLE

Published by ibooks, inc.:

THE "RAY BRADBURY PRESENTS" SERIES

Dinosaur World
Dinosaur Planet
Dinosaur Samurai
Dinosaur Warriors
Dinosaur Empire
Dinosaur Conquest
[coming April 2005]

The Best of Ray Bradbury:
The Graphic Novel
by Ray Bradbury, et. al.

Dinosaur Tales
by Ray Bradbury

RAY BRADBURY
PRESENTS

DINOSAUR EMPIRE

A NOVEL BY

STEPHEN LEIGH AND
JOHN J. MILLER

Illustrated by
Nicholas Jainschigg and Cortney Skinner

DISTRIBUTED BY SIMON & SCHUSTER, INC.

A Publication of ibooks, inc.

An ibooks, inc. Book

Distributed by Simon & Schuster, Inc.
1230 Avenue of the Americas, New York, NY 10020

ibooks, inc.
24 West 25th Street
New York, NY 10010

The ibooks World Wide Web Site Address is:
www.ibooks.net

ISBN 0-7434-9781-3
First ibooks, inc. printing November 2004
10 9 8 7 6 5 4 3 2 1

Printed in the U.S.A.

To my grandmother, Stella Pacion, with love
And to the memory of my grandfather, John Pacion

CONTENTS

PROLOGUE

It began on a warm summer day in the forest outside of Green Town, Illinois, when Aaron Cofield and his girlfriend Jennifer Mason found a clutch of dinosaur eggs.

An astonishing find for the budding paleontologist, it was just the beginning of their amazing adventure. While photographing the eggs with their friend Peter Finnigan, they help an injured man escape from a rampaging allosaurus. They take the man back to Aaron's house, where he tells his story.

His name is Travis. He's a time safari guide from two hundred years in the future. While hunting in the Mesozoic for a Tyrannosaurus Rex, a man named Eckels blundered off the temporal roadway. When the hunting party returned home the time-travelers found their history changed—for the worse. In a rage, Travis attacked Eckels. Eckels fled for his life in the time machine. The machine met itself in the Mesozoic and the resulting paradox caused an explosion that destroyed the temporal pathway.

Travis pursued Eckels in another machine. He came upon the wreckage as well as a marauding allosaurus. He leapt upon a piece of the broken temporal roadway to escape the dinosaur and found himself in Aaron's backyard.

Travis lapses into unconsciousness and ultimately disappears when left unattended by the teenagers. As they search for him Aaron literally falls on a section of the broken temporal roadway—and finds himself with Travis and the body of a dead T-Rex in the Mesozoic. Jennifer and Peter find a section of the path themselves, and Jennifer insists they go after Aaron. Peter reluctantly agrees and they are transported to a lush, junglelike forest. They find a trail of human footprints leading into a cave, where they're ambushed by Eckels. Eckels ties them up as he raves about talking dinosaurs and other nonsense. He leaves the cave, telling the two that he's going to offer them to the dinosaurs. While he's away, Jennifer and Peter escape, only to be captured by a group of sentient, man-sized dinosaurs armed with spears.

At the dinosaur village they're watched over by a female dinosaur named SStragh (the closest the humans can come to pronouncing her name is Struth). Jennifer and Peter learn that the vegetarian, rather peaceful Mutata (as the dinosaur tribe is called) have been recently troubled by invasions from what they call the "Floating Stones" (obviously bits of temporal roadway) and someone they call the "Far Killer." The Gairk, another tribe of sentient dinosaurs descended from carnivorous ancestors, are also searching for this "Far Killer."

Struth captures the Far Killer—who turns out to be Eckels. Eckels claims that he didn't ambush Peter and Jennifer. Jennifer doesn't trust him, though Peter falls under his fast-talking influence. The three plot to escape the Mutata, though Jennifer holds back after she develops a friendship with Struth.

Struth is an outsider among her own people. The Mutata are a society very much set in their ways. They follow a half-instinctive body of rules called the OColihi or "Ancient Path," which has been threatened by the recent disruptions that coincided with the arrival of the Floating Stones. Struth questions blind obedience to the OColihi, but her rebellion rarely goes beyond questioning into action.

Frraghi (or "Fergie"), the leader of the Mutata, want the humans killed, as do the Gairk. While in a confrontational conference about the fate of the humans, a strange storm strikes. Lightning flashes illuminate shifting patches of other realities, other timelines. A Gairk is killed as the storm moves right across where he is standing and transports half of him to another reality. Frightened, and believing that the humans somehow cause the storms, Fergie orders them killed. Struth cannot bring herself to disobey direct orders from the keeper of the OColihi.

Meanwhile, back in the Mesozoic, Aaron has to deal with an injured and rather unstable Travis. They take the time machine to Travis's "present," where they find only a desolate, cold waste. Travis concludes that Eckels has destroyed all of human history. Aaron eventually convinces Travis to try to return to Aaron's own hometime.

The world they go to is much like the world they just left. Aaron is shattered. His entire past is gone. Eckels has destroyed the timestream entirely. He's changed the past so much that nothing is the same.

The two despondent humans are suddenly attacked by a whirlwind, a vortex of pure force, which they learn is an extension of the world-mind, a consciousness that spans all living creatures in this world. They call him Mundo. Aaron convinces Mundo to join them as they return to the Mesozoic to capture Eckels.

Mundo puts himself into the body of a passing apelike creature. The trio return to the past. The trip proves very difficult for Mundo as for the first time part of him becomes disconnected from the greater whole. Mundo recovers and eventually they find the section of broken path and step on it. Surprised, Aaron finds himself in the forest near Green Town. Mundo runs away in anger, thinking that Aaron has tricked him. Aaron heads for his house, where he sees his Grandpa Carl standing on the porch.

But this is not "his" Green Town. The house is run down, Grandpa Carl is acting strange and irritable, and, worst of all, Aaron discovers that twelve years have passed in this world and his parents are dead.

He decides to go into town and discovers that Green Town itself has changed for the worse. Aaron meets an ex-schoolmate who's now thirty years old. Aaron flees when the man becomes suspicious of him, only to discover two agents from the quasimilitary establishment called the compound waiting for him back at the house. As Aaron watches from the woods Mundo approaches the house and Captain Michaels, the female agent, shoots at him. Mundo runs into the woods and Aaron follows him.

He doesn't find Mundo but he does discover the roadway that leads to the Mesozoic. Aaron returns to the past to find Travis, while back at the house Carl is arrested.

Travis tries an experiment with the time machine and discovers that he can't go any further UpTime than the present. This means that this version of Green Town is not Travis's past at all, but an alternate reality. They realize that the pieces of roadway cross not only time, but also various shadow worlds where history has taken other turns.

Aaron convinces Travis to send the time machine back to just after the Compound agents took off after Mundo. They materialize and see Carl put into a car.

Aaron is wounded in the ensuing confrontation, but he and Travis escape in the time machine.

Carl is taken to the Compound, but also manages to evade Michaels. He escapes via the piece of temporal roadway the authorities have found—the piece that had taken Jennifer and Peter to the Dinosaur World. He steps on it and disappears.

Meanwhile, in the Dinosaur World, the Mutata are continually bothered by attacks from two Floating Stones. Even more persistent—and bloodthirsty—than the samurai invaders are the huge pteorosaurs (called "saorod" by the Mutata), intelligent flying dinosaurs that strike mercilessly from the sky.

The presence of Peter and Jennifer affects the entire Mutata community. The Gairk leader issues his own declaration: the humans must die or the Gairk will declare war on the Mutata.

Struth eventually discovers the piece of roadway that Peter and Jennifer used to enter her world. While taking Jennifer to view it for confirmation, they run across a Gairk who tells them that he has just killed a "soft, pale thing" like Jennifer. The Gairk guides them to the spot and Jennifer recognizes the body.

It's Aaron's grandfather, Carl.

When Aaron returns to consciousness they're still at the farmhouse in Green Town, but several months in the future. Travis brought them there to spend a couple of weeks recuperating from their wounds. They're barely healed when Travis and the time machine are captured by agents from the Compound. Aaron manages to escape into the woods where he meets up with Mundo. They form an uneasy alliance and decide to rescue Travis.

Back on the Dinosaur World, Peters and Eckels eventually escape from the Mutata village, though Jennifer remains a captive.

In Green Town, Aaron, Travis, and Mundo discover that Captain Michaels is more sympathetic than they'd realized. She tells them that their scientists discovered that the gateways are powered by fragments of temporal mechanism embedded in the pathways by the explosion that occurred when Eckels's machine met itself. Take the fragments away and the gateway is sealed; put them back and it reopens.

Grateful to their unexpected ally, Aaron, Travis, and Mundo return to the Dinosaur World via the proper piece of roadway. Peter and Eckels, meanwhile, have holed up in Eckels's old cave, though their cover is blown when a party of Gairk hunters track Peter to the cave. Peter and Eckels escape out of a natural chimney in the cave's rear. Peter nearly falls from the top of a steep fissure when he reaches the end of his strength, but Mundo grabs him in time and hauls him up the last few feet. The reunion between Peter and the others is cut short as they hear the distinctive sound made by the time machine while in local travel mode. Eckels, who had preceded Peter out of the chimney, has stolen the vehicle.

Jennifer and Struth are searching for Peter and Eckels when they see the Gairk named Klaido rush past. Following him, they find themselves near the Floating Stone that leads to the world of the samurai. They watch Eckels drive the time machine over the Floating Stone into the other world, and are then reunited with the other temporal castaways who are hot on Eckels's trail.

They all follow Eckels through the portal and find themselves in the interior of a small, Shinto-like shrine. Eventually they are met by a group of samurai led by Captain Otomo. Having no choice, they surrender to Otomo, who takes them back to his walled village. The land is wild and untamed, but the general topography hasn't changed. They are in Illinois, near a nonexistent Green Town.

Struth comes through the portal later than the others, who are already gone when she emerges. She follows Eckels's path through the forest, but both are captured by a group of local Indians called the Hill Makers.

Aaron and the others are presented to Lord Akira. Mundo, both because of his resemblance to the Japanese mythological creature called the Monkey King and because he can use his telepathic powers to instantly learn Japanese, impresses Akira. He wheedles his way into the Lord's favor. Mundo discovers that a "dragon" has been spotted near the Hill Maker settlement and that Lord Akira greatly desires to own said dragon. Mundo begins to plan.

Jennifer, meanwhile, has told Aaron about his grandfather's death. The bad news steels Aaron's resolve and he vows to find a way to fix the mess Eckels has made.

Mundo contacts Grey Raven, head of the Hill Makers. He trades Japanese muskets for Struth. Aaron and Travis, working through Captain Otomo (who is not fond of Akira), learn that Struth has been brought to the castle.

Mundo, though, isn't quite done. Learning that Eckels is a prisoner of the Hill Makers, he goes to the Indian village and tells Eckels that he'll free him in exchange for the time machine. Eckels, always one to look out for his own skin, agrees.

By now, however, Lord Akira has also learned of the time machine. The Hill Makers and samurai fight for possession of the vehicle. In the middle of the fight Eckels realizes that the Hill Makers are going to lose, so he quickly changes sides.

Aaron and the others learn that Akira plans to rise to fame from what he considers his banishment to this miserable little outpost on the edge of civilization. He plans to take the time machine (or "Steel Turtle"), Mundo, and Struth, back to the settled territories of the west coast, and eventually return to the Imperial Court itself, back home in Nippon.

With Captain Otomo's grudging help the temporal castaways steal the time machine. At the shrine in the woods they deal with Akira and flee back through the Floating Path. Aaron and Travis close the gateway by removing the bit of temporal machinery embedded in the path. A glittering barrier rises up, and Aaron and Travis leap through the collapsing portal and return to the Dinosaur World.

They find an unfriendly welcome awaiting them. Fergie still wants the humans dead. The castaways escape—along with Struth—and enter the world of the Saorods, the intelligent, winged pterosaurs who've been making life miserable for the Mutata by endless attacks from their bit of temporal roadway. Aaron and the others manage to close off that temporal portal, and escape to yet another world.

They discover that this timeline is dominated by an Aztec-like culture. The Aztecs are fierce and unfriendly warriors, though the travelers are befriended by a priest named Tezozomoc. He helps them escape the spears of his own people, but extracts a promise from Aaron to find and rescue Chantico, the woman he loves. Chantico had gone through a temporal roadway some months ago, utterly vanishing.

Aaron goes through the portal last, deactivating the gate just before the spears of the Aztec warriors can find his heart. He jumps through at the last second, following his friends into the unknown . . .

LOST AND ALONE

Aaron Cofield didn't know what was worse, the cold that stabbed at him like hundreds of icy daggers or the nausea that threatened to make him mess up the front of his already filthy shirt. He grimly held out against both. He knew that neither would last long.

By now Aaron was a seasoned time-traveler. He wasn't comfortable with the sensations caused by moving through time, but he'd experienced them often enough to realize they didn't last long. He'd soon be through the frozen vortex of no-time and the cold and nausea would go away.

And then his real troubles would begin.

At that cheerful thought the unseen ground suddenly slammed him with enough force to knock his breath away. He opened his watering eyes and puffed a few times to get his lungs working again. He spat gritty grains of sand from his lips, wiped them from the palms of his hands. He groaned as unexpected and unaccustomed heat smashed him like a hammer.

Aaron looked around. Where was he? Even more important, *when* was he? He'd gone through the temporal portal only a few minutes after his friends. But time flowed at different rates on the different timelines. What was a few minutes on the Aztec world might be hours, days, or even weeks here. At any rate, something peculiar must have happened. His friends were nowhere in sight.

Aaron was the only living thing in a barren, baking landscape of gravel beds, sand, and stone outcrops. He turned in a circle and saw only an endless plain whose monotony was broken infrequently by battered ridges of sun-flaked stone or crescent-shaped sand dunes. There was nothing but sand, stone, and sun.

Aaron took a deep breath, and the hot desert air speared into his lungs, starting him coughing. He glanced at the sky and had to look away quickly. It was a cloudless, pale blue. The glare was blinding. The fierce, white-hot sun was a shimmering, indistinct circle. It wasn't even noon.

Aaron realized that he was in serious trouble. Of course, he had the bit of temporal machinery that opened the gate into the Aztec world, though returning there wasn't a viable option. Before activating the temporal mechanism he'd seen his only ally, Tezozomoc, overwhelmed by the knives and spears of their mutual enemies. Other Aztec warriors had been hard on Aaron's trail, their obsidian-tipped spears eager for Aaron's blood.

He couldn't go to any of the other worlds. The bits of machinery that opened those gates were in the hands of his friends. He was stuck in the middle of a nameless desert without food, proper clothing, or most importantly, water. There were no landmarks. He had no idea where his friends were. There was just the bit of temporal roadway, floating like a black shadow above a sea of shattered rock and sand . . .

Sand . . .

Aaron looked down at the ground. The area around the portal was lousy with tracks, human boots and sneakers, the prints of Mundo's bare feet, and Struth's clawed spoor.

Aaron wished that he was a skilled tracker like Travis. Travis could not only follow this trail easily, he could also tell exactly who made what tracks and probably how much weight everyone was carrying. Aaron could just tell that they were tracks. He watched the breeze obliterate some of them. If a stiff wind came up the trail wouldn't last for very long.

Aaron couldn't decide if he could afford to wait. It would be easier to travel at night without the awful heat dragging at his every step, but would the trail last that long? And how could he follow it in the dark?

Suddenly something in the desolate landscape caught Aaron's attention. He laughed. His friends may have gone off without him, but they'd left a message.

He took a deep breath. "Well," he said aloud, just to hear the sound of a human voice in the vast desolation around him, "guess I better get going. After all, the longest journey starts with the first step . . ."

He stepped on the trail left behind by his friends.

Peter Finnigan had come over first from the Aztec world. One moment he'd been filled with desperation as the Aztec warriors charged at them with obsidian-tipped spears, then, after the usual bout with frigid motion sickness, relief came with the realization that he was free and clear.

He stumbled off the piece of temporal roadway to make room for the others, and landed in a patch of coarse sand that was radiating so much heat that it was as warm as an overworked toaster.

It was a moonless night. The only light came from the stars shining far overhead. The air was cool. Peter remembered reading somewhere that deserts chilled rapidly with nightfall. He thought that it must be pretty early in the evening because the sand under his feet was still hot. The air cooled perceptibly as he waited. And waited. And waited.

He started to fidget. It was taking much too long. By now someone else should have followed him. He was peering closely at the bit of temporal roadway and wondering what he should do when with a snap, crackle, and pop of dissipating energy Jennifer Mason suddenly stumbled forward into his arms.

He caught her with a surprised "Oooofff," and they both fell backward onto the sand. She was a welcome weight in his arms. Jennifer had a slim, strong body and a long sheaf of blond hair that had grown unruly during the course of their adventures. Peter liked her, a lot. Once she had been his girlfriend and it bothered him more than a little that she was now Aaron's girl. It bothered him so much, in fact, that the former best friends were now adversaries.

"Thanks for the catch," Jennifer said as she got to her feet.

"No problem," Peter said. "What kept you?"

"Kept me?" Jennifer asked. "I jumped through the gate right after you. Couldn't have been more than a second or two."

Peter shook his head. "Something's screwy. I waited for you for . . . well . . . it felt like a pretty long time."

"Great." Jennifer sat down on a hummock of sand, frowning. "It looks like we're facing a major time differential between these worlds. A second or two versus, what, minutes? Hours?"

"Hard to say," Peter said. "An hour. Maybe more. It's difficult to tell without a watch."

"Hmmmm," Jennifer said. "I've been here about two minutes already. We can count off the seconds until someone else shows up."

"Great," Peter muttered. "That sounds exciting."

Jennifer nodded. She knew that Peter had little patience and no head for details. He was impetuous and headstrong. This didn't make him a bad person, but during the course of their adventures Jennifer had learned the importance of patience and caution.

"Exciting or not," she said. "It may turn out to be important. So . . ."

"So . . ." Peter said, "one thousand one, one thousand two—"

Jennifer nodded approvingly. "We'll take turns counting." She smiled. "It'll make the time go by faster."

"Sure. One thousand six. One thousand seven . . ."

They reached one thousand three-seven-five-oh before Eckels appeared in a blaze of sparks.

"An hour, maybe more," Jennifer said.

"Good to see you too," Eckels huffed. "What are you talking about?"

"How long it took you to come through the portal."

Eckels nodded. He was a scheming, self-centered coward, but he was no fool. He understood the implications of Jennifer's statement instantly. "Time differential, eh?" He looked around disapprovingly. "We're in for a long night."

He was right.

Travis came through next. By then, there was a distinct chill in the air and all the warmth had been sucked from the sand. The Aztec world had been warm, perhaps not as warm as this world might be in the daytime, but the temperature differential had been smaller. The travelers had been in a tropical climate for quite awhile and weren't used to the cold.

When Mundo came through the gate he found the four humans huddled together, trying to conserve their body warmth. Mundo's apelike body was covered with fur, so the cold didn't bother him. He looked around curiously.

"Any idea where we are this time?" he asked.

Peter shook his head. "None. You're welcome to look around if you like." He shifted uneasily. The chest wound he'd taken in the Nipponjin world was aching with the cold. "We have another hour to wait for the big lizard. Then for however long it'll take Aaron to come through."

Jennifer looked at Peter disapprovingly. " 'The lizard,' as you call her, is named Struth."

Actually, her name wasn't Struth, but that was as close as human vocal apparatus could come to pronouncing it. She and Jennifer were as close to friends as their different mental capabilities allowed. Peter—and also Eckels—had less friendly feelings toward the intelligent dinosaur. Struth was something of a rebel among her tradition-bound species. The other Mutata blamed the humans for the ravaging timestorms associated with the temporal roadways. They were under a death sentence from both the Mutata and their vastly more aggressive cousins, the carnivorous Gairk.

"Struth, Smuth. I hope it just gets here quick. Aaron too. Then we can get the heck out of here."

"And go where?" Travis asked quietly.

Peter had no reply.

"Well," Mundo said into the silence that threatened to stretch out for an uncomfortably long time, "maybe I'll take a look around."

"Don't go too far," Travis said. Travis was logically suited to be their leader, but as his wounds took more and more of a toll on his vitality, he was relinquishing that role to Aaron. He was anxious for Aaron to link up with them again.

"Don't worry about me." Mundo grinned fiercely, his fangs gleaming in the starlight. Despite his fierce appearance Mundo was more of a talker than a fighter. As a world-spirit he had been virtually immortal. Now that he was trapped in a body he was afraid that death might be unpleasantly permanent. Normally his actions were conservative beyond the point of cowardice and he looked out for himself first, second, and last. But also he was showing signs of accommodating to his new situation. He was learning more about emotions and becoming less self-centered. Travis still didn't entirely trust him, though. The fact that Mundo could read minds—or at least the thoughts on their surface—somehow made him seem even less trustworthy. Especially to Eckels, who had more secrets to hide than most.

Mundo was still on his scout when Struth arrived through the gate, clutching her spear awkwardly in her bandaged, three-fingered hands. Struth was taller than the humans. If she stood upright she would have been eight feet tall, but normally she leaned forward so her head was about six feet above the ground. Her scaled skin was a pebbly emerald color that shifted hues with her mood, well-being, and even as part of her language. Much stronger than the humans, she carried herself with delicate grace on massive hind-legs, using her long, whiplike tail to help keep her balance. Her forelimbs ended in clever, usually dexterous hands that were now encumbered by bandages because of injuries she sustained in the Aztec world.

"Jhenini!" she bleated. Her vocal apparatus wasn't entirely suited for any human language, but the two were comrades and companions if not exactly friends. The Mutata OColihi, their Ancient Path, had no place for the concept of "friendship," but Struth's whole life had been a struggle against the confinements of the OColihi.

She looked around. She would have shivered if she

could. The Mutata weren't cold-blooded, but they needed the warmth of the sun to function properly. If it got cold enough, Struth would slow down until she lapsed into comalike hibernation. If it got too cold she would never wake up.

"This is a terrible land," she said in the bleating, nasal language of the Mutata. Her posture, coloring, and scent also showed her discouragement.

Jennifer patted her slender neck in a gesture of appeasement.

"It's night, Struth. It'll get warmer in the morning."

Mundo came back from the darkness. "Nothing out there that I could see. No lights, no buildings, no nothing."

Eckels clamped his knees tightly to his chest. "We could start a fire. If there was anything to burn."

"Don't worry," Travis said, eyeing him sourly. "You won't freeze. I hope."

The two men stared at each other with mutual hatred.

"You won't," Jennifer said with as much authority as she could muster. Aaron usually kept the two from each other's throats. She hoped she could fill his role until he turned up. "It'll be uncomfortable, but we'll manage. We'll figure things out when the sun rises."

"*If* the sun rises on this world," Mundo said cheerfully. "Why, there's many strange timelines where the nights last for days, weeks even. On some the sun never—"

"Oh, shut up," Eckels said sourly.

"The sun will rise soon enough," Jennifer said with more confidence than she felt. "And Aaron will join us. Then we'll decide what to do."

"Sure," Peter said. But he spoke without real enthusiasm. "Aaron will know what to do."

Even Struth recognized the sarcasm that laced Peter's words. Jennifer had no strength to fight it. Struth curled up on the ground to take what warmth she could from the cooling sand. Jennifer leaned into the hollow of her rounded body to wait out the night and Aaron's arrival.

MARCH OR DIE

Dawn came quickly in the desert. At first Jennifer and the others welcomed the sun. It had become quite cold during the night. Even Mundo, despite his thick pelt, had felt the chill creep into his bones and had huddled with the others. Sleep had been infrequent and light. Struth had suffered the most and it took her several minutes to revive from her cold-induced torpor.

"I'm glad *that's* over for now," Peter said, stretching cramped muscles. "I never thought I'd be so happy to see the sun."

Eckels grunted sourly. "You'll be cursing it before the day is over. In case you've forgotten, we have no food, water, or shelter. It's going to be a *great* day."

"At least we're alive," Travis said. "And together."

"Except for Aaron," Jennifer reminded them.

"Yes," Travis said quietly. "Except for Aaron."

He hadn't appeared during the night and everyone was starting to feel more than a little anxious.

"Well, look," Peter said. "There's the time differential. We all left the Aztec world only a second or two apart, yet it took almost an hour for each of us to arrive. What if Peter were delayed for a minute or more?"

"It's hard to say," Jennifer said, calculating in her

head. "Maybe he'd take a day to come through. Maybe two."

"Maybe more," Eckels said. "And maybe he never even made it across."

"What are you saying?" Jennifer asked angrily.

"I'm saying we have to look out for ourselves," Eckels replied. "We have to find food. We're going to need water desperately. We can't sit around on our duffs and wait for Aaron to maybe show up."

"We're not going to abandon him," Jennifer said firmly.

She looked at Peter for support, but Peter turned away. She looked at Travis, who was frowning.

"Well . . ." the guide said slowly, "I hate to say it, but Eckels has a point. We're not going to do anyone any good if we all just sit around and die of thirst. We've got to get supplies."

"We can't desert Aaron," Jennifer repeated.

"You're right," Travis said, "and we won't. But we have to be practical. I've had some experience in the desert. It's an unforgiving environment. We can go a couple of days without food, but much more than a day without water will kill us all. For all we know there might be an oasis, or even a town, just out of sight. We have to get food and water. Otherwise no one will survive."

"All right," Jennifer said. "I understand what you're saying. You go look for water. I'll wait for Aaron."

Travis shook his head slowly. "That's no good, Jenny. It's too dangerous to split up like that. We don't know where or when we are. We have to stay together."

She looked around. For once, the group seemed to be in agreement. Struth, who had managed to follow most of the conversation, flared her nostrils in distress. She emitted the odor of rotting fruit that showed she was troubled.

"Struth?" Jennifer asked.

"I believe we should stick together, Jhenini," the dinosaur said. "It is the proper thing to do. But," she added, "I will stay with you if you want me to."

Jennifer put her hand on Struth's neck, touched by her offer. After a moment she shook her head. "No, you're right. We have to stick together. But we come right back here the moment we find water."

"Sure," Peter said. He looked at the others. "Agreed?"

"Agreed," Travis said firmly.

"Certainly," Mundo said, a shade too quickly.

"Of course," Eckels said, but no one believed him.

"All right." Jennifer glanced at the sun. It had barely cleared the horizon, but it was already very hot on her face. It promised to be a very warm day. She bent over and picked up a handful of sand, letting it trickle between her fingers. "If we leave a clear trail for Aaron, maybe he'll be able to follow us."

"Too bad we're out of bread crumbs," Eckels said with a barely concealed sneer.

"I've hunted in deserts before," Travis said. He gestured all around them. "These gravel plains are a common feature. The Arabs call them *regs*. There should be plenty of sand sheets on which we can leave a clear trail that'll last for weeks, months, even years. As long as there aren't any windstorms."

"If only we could leave Aaron a message," Jennifer said, half to herself. She suddenly looked up and snapped her fingers. "I've got it! Rocks! We'll use them to spell out a message."

Travis nodded. "That'd work."

"Okay," Jennifer said. "Which way do we want to go?"

The guide turned in a circle. The desert landscape looked identical in all directions. He shrugged.

"Hard to say which direction would be best. How about we head directly for the rising sun? That way we'll know we're going due east and we can use the sun's position to make sure we don't wander around in a circle."

"Right," Jennifer said. She looked around, then pointed to the side of a small, crescent-shaped sand dune. "We'll put our message there, on the side of the dune. Let's all gather some stones."

Mundo looked skeptical and Eckels grumbled, but they all pitched in. It took less than half an hour to gather enough rocks to spell out their message in letters two feet high.

FOLLOW, it read, with an arrow pointing due east.

"That's that," Travis said, wiping the sweat off his brow. "We'd better get going before it gets much warmer."

Jennifer took one last look at the piece of temporal roadway, hoping against hope that Aaron would suddenly appear in a shower of crackling energy. But he didn't.

She sighed. "Okay," she said, and they moved off together into the desert.

It was the hardest day of Jennifer's life. By noon she was completely exhausted. The sun beat on them. There were no clouds in the sky nor a hint of shade anywhere in the landscape. The dry air seared their lungs and snatched all the moisture from their bodies. Their mouths dried out almost immediately. Their tongues grew thick and swollen, their lips blistered and cracked.

The gravel plain rolled and dipped slightly, so that the horizon never seemed to be more than a mile away. When they reached one horizon, the next would be like the last: an endless expanse of nothing.

After a few hours of walking they came upon what looked like a group of fallen columns half buried in the sand. It fueled hope that they were getting close to some outpost of humanity, but when they hurried up to the columns they were astonished to discover they were actually the fallen trunks of petrified trees. The amount of detail in the fossilized logs was amazing. They could even see huge knots where branches had once grown out of the trunks.

"What do you make of it?" Jennifer asked Travis.

The wilderness expert shook his head. "Not much. Once the climate must have been wetter. There were trees, grass, water . . . it's all gone now, though."

Eckels sank down, collapsing on ground that was as hot as the bottom of a roasting pan, but he was so exhausted that he didn't care.

"That's it," he mumbled through cracked lips. "I've had it."

"Come on," Travis croaked in a voice full of disgust. "Get up. Get up or we'll leave you here to die."

"You'd like that, wouldn't you?" Eckels snarled.

Travis passed a hand over his head. His face and scalp had already been burned red by the fierce rays of the sun. "I wouldn't mind," he said wearily.

Jennifer bent down. "Come on," she said, tugging at Eckels's arm. She looked up at Peter. "Give me a hand, will you?"

Peter sighed. He barely had enough strength to keep himself going, but he couldn't let Jennifer see that. "Let's go, Eckels, or I'll kick your butt from here to . . . to wherever the heck we're going."

"Leave me alone," Eckels whined, trying to pull away from the two.

"Hey!" Mundo interrupted, excitedly pointing. "Look!"

"What's that?" Jennifer asked.

Travis squinted against the sun. "It's a ridge. A rock outcrop or something." It was difficult to see because of the shimmering heat waves rising from the sand. "There'll be shade. We'll be able to rest there until the sun goes down."

"What are we waiting for?" Peter said. "Let's go."

The party headed toward the rock outcrop. Even Eckels, complaining every step, struggled to his feet and staggered toward the ridge that cut through the shifting sands.

It wasn't much. Just a thirty-foot-high pile of sunburnt rock. But it did cast shade over the hellish landscape, and the time-travelers gratefully threw themselves into it. Even Struth crouched in its protecting shadow lest the continual heat overwhelm her body's defenses.

They lay waiting for the coolness of the evening, dreaming of tall glasses of iced tea and swimming pools filled with clear, crystalline water.

The afternoon passed like a fever dream. The heat was scorching. It would have killed them all if they'd tried to hike through it. The hours passed like years and at last the sun dropped below the horizon. It vanished with astonishing speed. One moment it was blazing like an out-of-control furnace. The next it was gone and night spread her dark cloak like a cool wave over the landscape.

They lay in the darkness, gathering strength. Everyone knew they had to find water, or die. But no one talked about it. Finally, when it was cool enough, they wearily rose and staggered away from the ridge that had sheltered them during the hottest part of the day.

They arrayed themselves for the evening's march. Mundo, with his superior night vision, was in the lead.

Just as they set off, something suddenly moved off to their right.

"What was that?" Peter asked.

They stopped. Whatever it was wandered back into sight.

"An antelope," Jennifer said.

"Gazelle," Travis said, more precisely.

It was a dainty, beautifully delicate creature. It pawed the earth not thirty yards away, then lowered its head to crop at the tuft of hard, dry grass it had found.

"Wish we had a rifle," Eckels said. "My stomach's rumbling. Maybe we can run it down."

"Maybe," Travis said judiciously. "If I wasn't already as dry as the plains of hell and hungry as a starving man."

Jennifer had been so thirsty she hadn't even thought of food. But the sight of the animal gave her hope.

"You know what this means," she said. "We must be getting close to water."

"She's right," Travis said. "This creature couldn't survive in the deep desert. We must be near its edge. Water can't be far away. Let's go."

They headed off into the night, their progress slow but steady. They followed the ridge that had sheltered them earlier. The walking was easier on its hard-packed, claylike surface. Jennifer followed Peter, who followed Mundo. There was no moon. Only the stars lit their way, so Jennifer had to keep looking to make sure she didn't twist an ankle tripping on one of the rocks strewn in their path. She was concentrating so hard on the footing that she walked right into Peter when he stopped in front of her.

"Hey! What—"

She looked up. Peter was staring straight ahead.

Mundo had also stopped, and was looking back questioningly at the humans.

"Are those mountains?" he asked, pointing at the horizon in front of them.

"No," Peter said.

"They're pyramids," Jennifer added.

They looked at each other and said at the same time, "Egypt."

"What?" Travis asked, pushing forward past Eckels, who had also stopped to stare.

"We're in Egypt," Jennifer turned to tell him.

"Say, Jennifer," Peter said in a strange voice. "Those are the Giza pyramids, right?"

"Right?"

"Aren't there *three* of them?"

"That's right," she said, frowning. "My gosh. There's only two."

"What are those lights?" Eckels asked.

"Lights?"

They all turned to look where he pointed.

"Well," Jennifer said, "it looks like a town."

Mundo licked blackened lips. "I hope they're friendly."

"I don't care if they're the devils of hell," Eckels said, pushing past. "I'm going to get some water."

"Good idea," Peter said. He followed Eckels.

Jennifer wanted to tell them to approach cautiously, but the thought of water and food suddenly overwhelmed her as well. She hurried after the others, toward the twinkling lights and whatever welcome they would bring.

THE ANCIENT CITY

The village dogs started barking well before they reached the edge of town as Jennifer wracked her brains for some kind of an explanation for Struth and Mundo. In the end she decided they'd just have to play it by ear. Fortunately, most of the people they'd run across didn't have much trouble accepting the group's two nonhumans. It helped that often their myths told of strange, powerful animals that sometimes were even gods.

The village was set at the base of a hill. One of the pyramids sat on the hilltop, the other was on lower ground a couple of hundred yards away. The village consisted of several hundred buildings. It was difficult to see any details in the dark. There were buildings clustered near but apart from the village, but these were without lights and seemingly without activity.

You couldn't say that for the village. By the time they'd arrived at its outskirts a welcoming committee consisting of twenty barking dogs and a dozen silent men with torches and weapons was waiting for them.

"Mundo," Jennifer called.

"I'm on it," he said, and advanced to the head of the group.

The villagers' torches were primitive burning

brands, but they cast enough light to reveal Mundo's inhuman features. Some mutters rose from the group and several of the men gripped their weapons more tightly, but none ran away screaming, or, more importantly, attacked the time-travelers.

Mundo held up his hands and spoke a few tentative words. He smiled, but that may not have been the best thing to do since his fangs glittered prominently in the torchlight.

"What are you saying?" Jennifer asked.

"Not much. Hello, friend, things like that. I can't get too much out of them until they start to speak."

"Are they friendly?" Eckels asked.

Mundo shrugged. "They haven't tried to spear us yet, have they?"

One of the men finally spoke. Their conversation was brief, but it seemed to satisfy him.

Mundo turned to the others and smiled. "They asked who we were. I said travelers from a far land. I told them we got lost in the desert and desperately need water and food. He's invited us into the village."

"All right!" Peter said.

The welcoming committee turned back toward the village, and the time-travelers followed. Travis sidled up to Jennifer and said quietly, "Notice something odd?"

Jennifer nodded. "Struth. They saw her, but no one even mentioned her. No one asked about her. I can see Mundo sliding by. He looks something like a man. But Struth is totally alien."

"Maybe," Travis said, "in this timeline she isn't."

"We'll see," Jennifer said.

There was a larger, somewhat more official-looking group waiting for them in the center of the village. At its head was a tall old man. He wore a long white skirt, or kilt, made of linen. He had a spotted leopard skin hanging from one bare shoulder as a short cape. He was lean, with wiry muscles. His head was shaved, except for a single braided scalp-lock. His face was stern, leaning toward grimness. Some of the men behind him had torches and were dressed and shaved like him. Others had weapons and the look of professional soldiers. Obvious villagers—men, women, and children—pressed in a rippling crescent around the welcoming committee.

"Welcome to our village," Mundo translated as the old man spoke. "My name is Rudjek. I am the high priest of the Ptah-Sokar-Osiris triad. Can we offer you water?"

Mundo nodded. "You bet. My name is Mundo. We're travelers from, uh, far away."

Rudjek shook his head, a small smile on his thin lips. "Indeed you are," he said, looking directly at struth. "Yet you speak our language quite well."

"Well," Mundo said. "I'm a fast learner. The others will take a little longer to pick it up."

As Mundo spoke one of the men dressed like Rudjek came out of the crowd bearing a large clay jar and a long-handled dipper. He put the jar down at his feet and offered Jennifer a ladle of cool, sweet water.

Jennifer took it, nodded and smiled. She sipped while Rudjek and Mundo continued to converse.

"The old bird is Rudjek," Mundo said after a moment. "He seems to be in charge. He's a priest. He says to take it easy on the water. There's as much as we need, but don't drink too fast."

"He's right," Travis said. "Drink too much too fast and your stomach won't be able to handle it."

"I know how to drink water," Eckels said, elbowing in front of Peter and grabbing the dipper.

"Hey!" Peter said.

Eckels shot him a nasty look.

"Choke on it," Peter muttered, and Eckels did, sputtering and spitting.

"You seem out of practice," Travis said dryly.

Eckels glared at him.

"All this talking is drying me out," Mundo said. "Pass the dipper, will you?" Mundo took a drink and smacked his lips. "Hmmm. Great stuff. Rudjek has suggested that we go to a more comfortable place where we can discuss things in private."

"I think that's a good idea," Jennifer said.

"Right." Mundo turned to the priest. "Lead on."

Rudjek gestured and the crowd that had gathered to watch the arrival of the time-travelers parted like the Red Sea. He led them to a walled estate on the edge of the village. Inside the wall was a central manor house and a number of outbuildings. None of the armed men followed them into the house, and most of the priests also dispersed into the darkness.

The house was dimly lit by torches and candles. They went through a central doorway, past a small, empty reception room to what seemed to be the house's main room. It was sparsely furnished with wooden benches and floor cushions, and was beautifully painted and immaculately clean. The plastered walls were whitewashed to about three feet above the floor, then painted a light red. A frieze depicting fruit and flower vines ran around the walls near the ceiling. The artwork was beautifully executed with many types of fruit and flowers, both exotic and familiar. The colors were vibrant greens, yellows, and blues. A single central pillar helped hold up the high ceiling. It was red-painted wood carved to look like a palm tree. The pillar's capital was carved like palm leaves and painted green.

It was a cool, pleasing room and Jennifer and the others gratefully collapsed on the cushions indicated by Rudjek. The priest didn't even bat an eye as Struth took a place near the wall. He spoke and Mundo translated for the benefit of the others.

"He says," Mundo relayed, "that he's arranged for drink and food to be bought."

"Great," Eckels said. "I'm starving."

"Mundo," Jennifer said with some concern, "can we trust this guy? I mean, he seems to be taking everything, us, you, even Struth, so calmly."

Mundo shrugged, a gesture he was becoming very adept at. "His mind is an open book, sincere, tranquil, honest. I can't detect any treachery. It's weird."

Travis smiled. "Oh, come now—"

He was interrupted as a strange figure burst into the room, half-dancing, half-skipping, and shouting at the top of his lungs, "Make way, make way, make way, for Tchay the Great! Queller of the Desert Savages, First Under the King, Beloved of Re! Great Nomarch and Protector of the People!"

The newcomer was a dwarf. His legs were short and bowed, but his chest was deep and his bare arms were heavily muscled. His hair was dark, his eyes were deep and beautiful. He was the first bearded man they'd seen in the village. He stopped his bizarre chant and turned to the doorway and bowed low, his forehead nearly touching the floor.

Two men entered the room. They were nearly naked and impressively muscled. Both carried stone-headed clubs. They automatically stepped to either side of the doorway as a third man entered.

He was nearly as tall as his bodyguards and nearly as muscular, though age had layered his muscles with fat and streaked his close-cut black hair with grey. He had an impressive face. It was hard, handsome, and cold with a great blade of a nose and eyes that seemed to be marble rather than mere flesh.

"Great Tchay!" the dwarf intoned solemnly.

Rudjek inclined his head, and Jennifer thought it prudent to follow course, as did all the other humans. Only Struth looked on without submission, her reptilian stare a match for the human's.

Tchay wasted no time trying to stare down the Mutata. He turned for the only unoccupied wooden bench. The dwarf scurried forward to place a cushion on his master's seat. Tchay started to lower his rump onto the bench, and, at the last moment, the dwarf snatched the cushion away.

Tchay plopped down the extra few inches and his butt nearly slipped off the bench. The dwarf roared with laughter and Rudjek's lips twitched in a barely suppressed smile.

Tchay scowled a scowl that might have frightened the gods in heaven and lashed out with a sandaled foot, catching the dwarf on his side. The dwarf rolled with the kick, somersaulted, and came up laughing.

"This," Jennifer said in a low voice, "is a man we'd better watch closely. Who is he, anyway?"

"He seems to be the local political authority," Mundo explained. "Far as I can figure, Rudjek is high priest and head of this community. This Tchay is the head of the political unit—they call them nomes—for this whole area."

"So he's more powerful than Rudjek?" Peter asked.

"I'd say so," Mundo said, then his attention was drawn to the high priest as Rudjek began to explain the situation to Tchay. As Rudjek was talking two underpriests came into the room bearing trays of food and drink. Everyone took food gratefully and ate and drank slowly, although they were ravenously hungry and as dry as the desert through which they'd trekked.

"Aaron!" Jennifer said suddenly, putting down a half-peeled orange. "We have to go after him."

Travis shook his head. "We can't, now. Not in the dark. Odds are, one man wandering around the desert, we'd miss him clean. We have to wait for first light."

Jennifer opened her mouth to protest, but realized that Travis was right. She took a bite of orange, feeling more than slightly guilty.

Rudjek finished his explanation and Tchay looked at them stonily. He barked out a short sentence, which Mundo translated to the surprise of them all.

"So," Tchay had said, "what time have you come from?"

Aaron was delirious by the time he reached the ruins of the ancient city.

He'd walked through the desert for half a day, most of the following night, and part of another day. He'd reached the limits of his endurance. His skin was blistered and peeling, his lips cracked and swollen. He had stopped sweating a long time ago because his body simply had no more moisture to spare. He was dangerously close to sunstroke.

Aaron's eyes closed to tiny slits against the incessant glare of the brilliant sun. They'd been playing tricks on him for some time now. The superheated desert air had clouded his vision and confused his baked brain a number of times. Sometimes he thought he saw distant hills promising cool shade among jumbled rocks. Other times clear, blue lakes shimmered out of reach. He almost didn't believe it when he saw the fallen columns awash in a sea of sand.

"Won't be fooled again," Aaron mumbled. He knuckled his half-closed eyes, rubbing the gritty paste from their corners. He opened them wide, instantly regretting it as the cruel sunlight stabbed deep into their sockets, seemingly scorching his brain. He shook his head and looked again at the fallen columns.

They were still there.

"Huh. Whaddaya know . . ."

He shambled forward, too far gone to even pick up his feet. He collapsed against the first column that he reached. He hugged it for a moment, though it was burning hot from the merciless sun. He lay against it, breathing heavily. He couldn't go on.

There was a deep black stain on the other side of the column. For a moment Aaron was baffled. He couldn't figure out what it was. Then it finally penetrated his fevered brain. It was shade. The first he'd seen all day. The sun was slipping down from its high point in the sky and the fallen column was thick enough to cast a foot or two of dark shadow.

It looked as cool and inviting as a bottomless swimming hole.

Aaron licked his cracked lips with his dry, swollen tongue. He wanted that shade. He needed it. He marshaled all of his strength and managed to heave one leg over the fallen column. He sat astride it for a moment. He grunted, got his body rocking, and let gravity do the rest. He slipped around the column and hit the ground like a limp rag doll.

"Shade," he told himself.

He closed his eyes and probably slept for a bit. He couldn't tell for sure. It was getting increasingly difficult to differentiate sleep from wakefulness from hallucination. He thought he dreamed. It was something about an ice cream float the size of a glacier. When he'd finished eating it and opened his eyes again it was still afternoon. The sun still blazed in the sky, but it was definitely a lot closer to the western horizon.

He blinked rapidly, astonished at what he saw in the ruins. A pond was nestled among the fallen columns. It was weird that he hadn't noticed it before and at first he thought it was another mirage. But it couldn't be. It lay tranquilly among the ruins of the city, and the ruins were real, that was for sure. So the pond had to be real, too.

Aaron pulled himself up to his knees and somehow managed to get to his feet. He staggered forward and the staggering turned into a teetering, off-balance run. It seemed that he would fall on his face with every step, but somehow he kept going.

Aaron grinned. He could smell the water now. He flung himself forward in an awkward, face-first dive and hit the water hard. He didn't care. He splashed, laughing out loud, making a horrible, croaking sound like laughter from a dehydrated frog.

As he splashed through the water he knew he was sinking deeper and deeper, but he didn't care. Part of his brain was alarmed, telling him that he could drown, but he didn't care. He wanted to stay underwater forever. It was funny that he was still thirsty, though.

From far away a sound came. It could have been someone calling his name, but he couldn't remember what his name was. He ignored the sound as he sank languorously in the warm pool.

Gentle hands touched him, turning him over. He squinted up at a hairy, bestial face out of someone's nightmare. He frowned. His brain laboriously put a name to the face.

"Mundo," he croaked. "Did you bring your bathing suit?"

Mundo looked up shouted, "Jennifer, he's here. I've found him!"

The creature held something to Aaron's lips. It bubbled out over his scorched face, running like a blessing over his blistered features. Some found its way past his swollen lips and he swallowed convulsively. The trickle of water was immediately absorbed by the dust that choked his throat.

Someone kneeled down by him, casting a shadow over his face.

"He was swimming in the sand," Mundo said. "Or was trying to, anyway."

"Oh, Aaron."

It was Jennifer. She was beautiful, like a cool angel. Aaron looked at her and smiled. He knew now that everything would be all right.

KEMET

Aaron slept for a long time. It was a light, fevered sleep, broken by pain and dreams, but everytime he woke someone was at his side. Usually it was Jennifer. Sometimes it was Travis or Peter. Once it was even Mundo who read his mind and held a glass of chilled fruit juice to his lips before he could even say anything.

Sometimes his friends were accompanied by strangers, clean-shaven men in white robes who looked on with concern. Aaron didn't think about it. He was just happy to be out of the sun in a cool, dark place, with plenty of water to drink.

Finally, he woke up coherent enough to wonder where he was and how he'd gotten there. He focused on the person sitting at his bedside. It took him a moment to realize that it was Jennifer.

"Hello," she said, and smiled.

"Hello." He knew there was something important he had to ask about, but it took a moment for his brain to chase it down. "The pieces of temporal mechanism—"

"Safe," Jennifer said. "All safe. We each carried a piece when we trekked out of the desert."

Aaron sighed with relief. He looked around the room, then back to Jennifer. "How did I get here?"

"Mundo found you trying to swim in a patch of sand."

"Sand?" He thought hard, trying to separate dream from reality. "I was in a pool of water. A pool in the ancient city."

Jennifer laughed. "There was no ancient city. What you thought were fallen columns were really petrified tree trunks. We thought they were ruins when we first saw them, too, but we caught on soon enough. You were delirious."

"Really? Petrified tree trunks . . . It all seemed so real."

"You were pretty far gone," Jennifer said. "Fortunately our hosts have a lot of experience in treating heatstroke."

"Our hosts . . . where are we, anyway?"

Jennifer smiled again. "A land called Kemet."

"Kemet?" Aaron frowned. "Never heard of it."

"Yes, you have. Only under the name the Greeks gave it: Egypt."

"Egypt . . ." Aaron sat up on his elbows. "Pyramids, mummies, the Nile? That Egypt?"

Jennifer nodded.

"I've got to see this." He started to throw off the white linen sheet that covered him, then stopped. "First, though, I'd better get some clothes."

"That," Jennifer said, "would be a good idea."

"This is it, huh?" Aaron said to the attendant as he held up the folded square of cloth.

The man looked down on him with a superciliousness that would have done an English butler proud. He repressed a sigh. He couldn't speak to Aaron, but somehow he managed to convey the method for wrapping and fastening the linen kilt that came down to Aaron's knees. A pair of sandals completed his outfit. That was it.

It felt good to be up and about. The servant led Aaron from the room where he'd recovered from his brush with sunstroke, through a pleasantly cool house that was spotlessly clean. The walls were plastered and whitewashed. Aaron didn't have too much time to dwell on architectural details, because Jennifer was waiting for him on a cushioned wooden bench in the next room.

She stood and hugged him. The servant permitted himself a slight smile, then glided away.

"Boy," Aaron said as they hugged, "I thought for awhile that I was never going to see you again."

"You can't get rid of me that easily."

Aaron held her at arm's length. "I like your outfit," he said.

She wore a long, almost floor-length linen dress that was tighter than his. She also wore a short-sleeved tunic that covered her upper body. A pair of sandals also completed her attire.

Jennifer smiled. "Well, it's somewhat more modest than what most of the women wear around here. You can't blame them. It's beastly hot. Still, you should see Peter's eyes bug out of his head when he sees some of the more, um, daring, outfits."

They'd linked arms and were walking as they talked, moving from the cool interior of the house into the heat of the day. It was early morning, but already quite hot.

"Did everyone else get through okay?" Aaron asked.

"Everyone's fine," Jennifer assured him. "Mundo is a little put out that the local pantheon seems to lack monkey gods."

Aaron laughed. "I'll bet. Say, Struth must have made quite an impression on the locals."

Jennifer smiled wryly. "In a way." She stopped and

pointed before Aaron could question her any further. "Look," she said.

He saw what she was pointing at, and gasped. They had passed through the village and were standing at the base of a hill. Atop it was a pyramid. Aaron had seen many pictures of its four-thousand-year-old state, but now it was whole, complete, and just recently finished. It shone in three colors. The bottom two-thirds was gleaming red granite. Above that was a strata of blinding white limestone, dazzling in the early morning sun. A thin sheath of gold leaf capped the upper twenty feet. The gold was blinding in the sun. It was a beautiful, awe-inspiring sight.

Behind this pyramid loomed another. This one, too, looked like it could have been finished yesterday. It appeared smaller than the first pyramid, but actually it was taller. It only seemed smaller because it sat on level ground while the closer pyramid was built on a hilltop. In front of the second pyramid was a field of smaller buildings dwarfed into insignificance by the overwhelming majesty of the two pyramids.

"Impressive, no?"

"Impressive, yes," Aaron said. "But weren't there three pyramids at Giza?"

Jennifer nodded. "There will be a third. When the next pharaoh builds it."

"You mean . . ."

Jennifer nodded again. "We seem to have landed fairly early in Egypt's history. I'm hardly an expert, but we're probably in about 2500 B.C. That pyramid"—she pointed to the further one—"was the first true pyramid. It was built by the Pharaoh Khufu. This one"—she gestured at the one in front of them—"was built by his son, Khafre. Who, as it happened, died about two months ago. The third pyramid will be built by *his* son, Menkaure."

"Then Khafre's entombed in his pyramid?"

Jennifer shook her head. "The funerary rituals take a long time, especially when a pharaoh's involved. There's still a few days before he'll be put into his burial chamber. But come on, there's something I want you to see."

She led the way down a path that led to a gap in the mudbrick wall enclosing the pyramid's precinct. They passed a number of workers scurrying on their daily rounds. It seemed everyone knew who they were, and no one was shy about greeting them. Jennifer returned their waves and hellos as they passed.

"What are those?" Aaron asked as the path took them closer to the buildings next to Khufu's pyramid.

"Tombs," Jennifer said. "Tombs of Khufu's nobles, advisors, and friends." They went through the gap in the enclosure wall. "We've been looking at the back of Khafre's pyramid. Let's cut across this way to get a view of the front."

They walked across dry, dusty ground, and came upon a columned building sitting before the pyramid.

"This is the mortuary temple where the priests will perform memorial services for Khafre until the end of time. Or at least as long as his dynasty stays in power" She pointed downhill. There were a number of other buildings in front of the pyramid. A covered causeway led from the mortuary temple to another building nestled at the base of the hill. "Look at that."

Aaron looked. The sight was breathtaking. Before him lay the Nile River. It flowed like a blue ribbon. The ground bordering the Nile was green, the first green that Aaron had seen in Kemet. There was grass and trees and flowers of a dozen different kinds. Facing the Nile, with his back towards them and his paws only a score of yards from the water, was a familiar being.

"It's the Sphinx," Aaron said.

"It is," Jennifer agreed. "Let's take a closer look."

They went down the causeway that connected the mortuary temple in front of the pyramid to another temple at the base of the hill, right next to the Sphinx.

The causeway had a flagstone floor. Its walls were decorated with colorfully painted scenes of Khafre dining, hunting ducks and geese on the Nile, and crushing enemies under his foot and with a stone war mace. It was crowded. The workmen scurrying to and fro had an organized air about them, as if they were members of a beehive where every bee knew its assigned task.

Aaron and Jennifer reached the end of the causeway after a stroll of a quarter of a mile. Aaron was sweating by the time they'd finished, and having uncomfortable memories of his recent ordeal in the desert. Jennifer seemed to sense his discomfort.

"It's not much farther," she said.

"I'm okay."

They reached the end of the causeway, which essentially was the back door of another structure.

"What's this building?" Aaron asked.

"According to Mundo the priests call it the Valley Temple." It sat right on the bank of the Nile, with a pier leading from its front door to the water's edge. "Khafre's being embalmed inside."

"Oh."

"This way," Jennifer said, leading them around the temple to a spot where they could look the Sphinx right in the eye. Aaron's curiosity was piqued, but he momentarily forgot about the stone monument when he saw Peter standing before it, staring at it broodingly.

"Peter!"

Peter turned to look at his onetime friend, and Aaron was happy to see genuine gladness in his eyes.

"Aaron!" He punched his fellow time-traveler lightly

on the arm. "Man, you had us worried for awhile. We thought you'd been turned into a french fry!"

"Nope," Aaron said. "Takes more than a stroll across a desert to do me in. Though I did get a little sunburned."

Peter laughed. "We all did. We were lucky to stumble across the village. It's a good thing we decided to go right instead of left when we got off the temporal roadway, or we'd all still be marching through the desert."

Jennifer shook her head. "I don't think we'd still be marching."

Aaron shrugged. "Let's not worry about it. We're all here and we're all okay. Now, what's this great mystery you want to show me."

Peter pointed at the Sphinx. "You're looking at it," he said.

Aaron frowned. For a moment he didn't get it. The Sphinx had been carved out of a limestone outcropping, not built there bit by bit. At first it looked just like the Sphinx. It looked somewhat odd, but that was because it was fresh, free from the battering of the passing millennia . . . No, Aaron suddenly realized, it was more than that.

It didn't have the familiar Sphinx face. It didn't have the face of a man. Its face was weird . . . reptilian. Yet it was also familiar. As impossible as it sounded, Aaron had seen that face before.

"Oh my God," Aaron said suddenly, quietly.

"Recognize it?" Jennifer murmured.

"Do I? It's Klaido." He suppressed a shiver despite the heat of the day. Klaido was a Gairk, a cousin of the Mutata. Both races had evolved from dinosaurs, but Struth's Mutata ancestors had been peaceful vegetarians and Klaido's had been ravening carnivores. Klaido wasn't kindly disposed to the humans. He had, in fact, vowed to kill them all on sight. He'd disappeared in a timestorm, caught up and transported to another world. Apparently this world.

"What does this mean?" Aaron asked after a long moment.

"I don't know," Jennifer said.

"But I doubt it's anything good," added Peter.

AN UNEXPECTED DINNER GUEST

Aaron was napping when Mundo came into his chamber and woke him for the evening meal.

"Come on," the ape said, shaking him gently. "You're not going to get any better laying around here all night. It's time to get some food into you."

Aaron yawned and sat at the edge of the bed, knuckling his still-sleepy eyes. "I'm starved," he said, then quickly added, "Oh. Who's this?"

Aaron realized for the first time that Mundo had a companion. It was a small man, a dwarf, in fact. His head was shaven, but he wore a full beard, the first Aaron had seen in Kemet. His short legs were thick and bowed, his short arms were ridged with muscle.

"This is Pawero," Mundo said. "He's Tchay's fool."

"Hello," Aaron said. He looked at Mundo. "Do they shake hands around here?"

Mundo shook his head. "Apparently that hasn't been invented yet." He turned to the dwarf and spoke in the ancient Kemet tongue.

The dwarf smiled broadly. He had beautiful white teeth. He said something in return, bowed deeply, and did a backflip, landing softly on his feet.

Aaron smiled. "Um, tell him that was really . . . something."

Mundo smiled sarcastically, exposing his fangs. "I'll try to make your response more enthusiastic."

"Sure," Aaron said. "You said he was a fool? You mean like a court jester?"

"Yeah," Mundo replied after he'd finished chatting with Pawero for a moment. "These Kemetians put a big store in dwarves. Apparently they're sacred to some of their crazy-looking gods. Pawero belongs to Tchay. He's the nomarch."

"Nomarch?" Aaron asked as they headed down the hall together.

"Yeah, nomarch. A nome is like a state or county. The nomarch's the governor."

"What's this Tchay like? Have you, well, examined him yet?" Even though Aaron had been around Mundo for awhile, it was difficult to get used to the creature's uncanny ability to read other's minds. It was a useful talent. For one thing it made Mundo an instant translator in whatever strange place they found themselves. Mundo could read mainly surface thoughts. He couldn't get into someone's deepest, darkest secrets, but it was still an odd, prying ability that Aaron never felt quite comfortable discussing.

"You mean read his mind?" Mundo asked flatly.

"Well, yeah."

"What do you take me for?" Mundo asked indignantly. "Of course I did. Right when we first met him. Our lives could depend on how we get along with this guy."

Aaron nodded. "Of course. I should have known. So what kind of guy is he?"

"Ambitious," Mundo said. "Very, very ambitious. Well, here we are."

Aaron decided to let his questions wait as they entered the banquet hall. Evidently this wasn't just a simple, private affair. It looked like all the local big shots had been invited.

The dining room was spacious, with a high, airy ceiling. There were a number of tables ranked about the room. Those at the front, on a low dais, were empty. Aaron's friends sat together at a table in the center of the room. Local dignitaries crowded around the others.

Pawero led the way into the hall. He strutted in an exaggerated, self-important manner. When everyone's eyes were on him he launched into a series of cartwheels, but, on the last one, landed heavily on his butt. He rubbed it hard, his face a mask of comic pain, and a ripple of laughter went through the hall.

He landed, Aaron noted, right in front of the other time-travelers. They were all present, even Struth, who, unable to use the human chairs, simply stood at her place, her tail curled around her feet. They all looked good, though as usual Eckels had a sour expression. Pawero suddenly sprung to his feet and indicated the empty places at the table where the time-travelers sat.

"That's our spot," Mundo said and led the way to the table, welcoming the attention of every person in the room.

Aaron felt less comfortable in the spotlight, but any sense of discomfort vanished when he greeted his friends again.

"Travis!" They shook hands warmly. "You're looking good."

"Feeling better. They've been taking good care of us."

"Struth." He rubbed the Mutata's neck like he'd seen Jennifer do, and was greeted by an incomprehensible blatt of noise and the smell of ripe citrus fruit as Struth adjusted her scent to that of welcoming. He hugged Jennifer and slapped Peter lightly on the shoulder as he sat between them. He even tossed Eckels a glance and a casual "Hello."

Eckels just grunted.

"Everyone's looking good," Aaron said.

"We're getting to be pros at this time-hopping business," Travis said.

"Everyone's been great to us," Peter said.

"So far," Eckels said sourly. "Who knows what they're planning?"

As much as Aaron hated to agree with Eckels on anything, the man was probably right. They'd dropped right into the middle of an alien society. They had to find their way home, eventually, but also Aaron had promised to find Chantico, the Aztec girl who had come into this world before them. Aaron had made the promise to Tezozomoc, the Aztec priest who had brought the time-travelers freedom with his life. And Klaido's presence was a wild card, a completely unknown but no doubt dangerous variable in the equation.

"Eckels is right," Aaron said. "Anyone know exactly what's going on here?"

There were mutters and shaken heads. Meanwhile, Pawero had gotten a trumpetlike instrument from somewhere and had blown a few notes on it that sounded remarkably like Struth's blatted nasal tones. All eyes turned to the back of the room as a full-scale procession entered the banquet hall.

First came a pair of girls littering the floor with flower petals. Aaron felt Jennifer's elbow dig into his ribs and realized that he was staring. He wasn't the only one. They were in a different time and in a different climate and what little the girls wore was appropriate for both. Still, *he* wasn't of this time, and the girls were very beautiful and wore very little. He turned to Jennifer and smiled weakly.

"Stop leering," she said, "like these other male chauvinist pigs." She gestured at Peter, Travis, and Eckels.

"I'm not—" he began, then realized this was not an argument that he could win. He turned back to watch the procession.

Next came the standard bearers, strong, muscular men who wore as little as the flower girls who had proceeded them. Behind them was a tall old man dressed all in white. His head and face were clean-shaven except for a long, braided scalp-lock. A massive ornament of gold and silver and blue stone covered his narrow chest. It was in the shape of a vulture with spread wings. Other amulets dangled around his neck, but they were insignificant compared to the huge pectoral. It looked like it weighed more than ten pounds. It was amazing that he bore up under the weight of it.

"That's Rudjek," Mundo whispered. "Here's the head priest of the mortuary complex and the Ptah-Sokar-Osiris cult."

"The what?" Aaron asked.

Mundo sighed. "It's complicated. Here's the short course. Egypt—Kemet, as the natives say—has literally hundreds of gods and goddesses. Most of them are local deities. When the country was unified by the early kings the gods and goddesses themselves sort of came together, often as triads. Kind of like three-god teams. Ptah is the god of craftsmen and artisans. Appropriate for this place. Some believe he even created man. Sokar is the death god. Also kind of appropriate. Osiris is maybe the most important god of all. He's the god of the dead—not death, the *dead*—and resurrection. Got all that?"

"Sure," Aaron said with a frown. "I guess."

"We can get into the symbolism later."

Three women came behind Rudjek. One was old, but of majestic and haughty bearing. The second was in her late thirties. She'd kept more of her beauty than the older woman, and was just as regal. The third was young, no more than Aaron's age, and, Aaron had to admit, one of the most beautiful women he'd ever seen. Her black hair fell in thick waves to her waist. Jeweled combs of silver and gold sparkled in it. More jewels glittered at her ears, neck, biceps, and wrists. Rings flashed on every finger. Her skin was as flawless and smooth as ivory. Her eyes were heavily made up with blue eye shadow and mascara. Her full, curved lips were painted red.

"Who's that?" Peter whispered.

"Uh-uh," Mundo said. "*That* is Kiya, Tchay's youngest wife. And his pride and joy. You'd better keep away from her if you know what's good for you."

"And that's Tchay?" Aaron whispered.

Tchay liked to make an entrance. He came last in the procession, except for the two attendants, unadorned but beautiful girls, who fanned him with luxurious ostrich-feather fans. He was tall and well built, his face was hard and imperious. He looked like he was used to giving orders and having them obeyed. Aaron was wary of him. Why he couldn't say. Aaron had met hard men before on his travels—Captain Otomo in the Japanese world sprang to mind—but this man was more than hard. He looked ruthless. And the only really ruthless men Aaron had ever met were like Eckels—totally concerned with only their own ends, totally self-absorbed, and totally untrustworthy.

"That's Tchay," Mundo said flatly.

Pawero had set aside his musical instrument and was skipping madly among the procession. He came right up to one of the flower girls and made a horrid face. She shrieked as he snatched the basket of petals from her and ran away as he tried to pinch her backside. Many of the assembled guests laughed as he joined the procession, imitating the other flower girl with mincing, exaggerated steps and movements.

When the party reached the dais he simply threw his bucket of petals at one of the tables. The other guests roared with laughter, though those picking flower petals out of their teeth didn't seem too happy.

Pawero ignored Rudjek, who sat at one end of the long table as the standard bearers arranged themselves behind it. Pawero went for the hand of Tchay's oldest wife. Not pleased, she batted his hand away and seated herself.

Pawero, now with a look of intense sadness on his amazingly agile face, took the hand of the middle wife. She deigned to let him lead her to her seat, but really took no notice of him.

The third wife, Kiya, smiled broadly at the dwarf. She took his hand without hesitation and they did sort of an intricate, impromptu dance to the head table. He seated her with a flourish and bowed low. She leaned forward and kissed him quickly on the forehead.

"Uh-uh," Mundo said. "I think our little friend has gone a touch too far."

Tchay's face grew harder, darker. Pawero seemed to take no notice. He danced up to the nomarch with a broad smile on his face and made no move to avoid the kick that he didn't see coming.

The blow caught him on the side. Pawero fell spinning on the polished floor and crashed into one of the dining tables. He upset a ewer of wine and it spilled, trickling down on his head.

There was total silence for a heartbeat and then sudden, booming laughter from Tchay. It took a moment, but the rest of the room joined in. Even Pawero smiled. He stood, grimacing.

"He may have a broken rib," Jennifer said, outraged.

She started to stand, but Aaron grabbed her arm and held her back.

"You can check him out later," he said in a low voice. "He seems okay for the moment."

Indeed, Pawero was standing, and, if moving about a bit gingerly, was clowning in front of Tchay again, bowing and scraping and leading him to his chair in the middle of the front table.

"It looks like our host is into slapstick," Travis said in a tight voice.

"Whatever he's into, he's in charge," Aaron said. "We have to walk softly until we discover what kind of land we're walking on."

"Well put," Eckels said silkily.

Tchay gestured imperiously from the front table and servants hurried forth with heaped platters of food. Aaron was starving. One thing he'd learned was to eat when food was available—and here was plenty. And it looked good.

The servants were about to set the first platters in front of them when a sudden commotion sounded in the back of the dining hall. Everyone turned to look, even Tchay, who had a thunderous frown on his face.

There was a massive roar and the sound of huge feet stomping on stone.

"I know that sound," Struth said quietly. "It is—"

"Klaido!" Eckels whispered in a frightened, strangled voice.

The killer dinosaur stomped into the room, his head swaying right and left, his mouth gaping open in a hideous grin that exposed rows of sharp fangs the size of daggers. He saw the time-travelers, stopped, and screamed a horrible challenge. Struth stood and faced her fellow dinosaur.

"The time is not now," she told Klaido. "We must return home to pass sentence on the humans."

Klaido flared angrily, his head whipping back and forth like a snake's.

"Do not attempt to order me about, Mutata weakling. I am a Gairk! When I see an enemy, I kill it!"

He took a ponderous step forward. Aaron stood, pushing in front of Jennifer. He looked around but nothing more lethal than a wooden spoon was close at hand.

"Better get ready to run," he said in a tight voice.

Klaido roared his challenge again, but before he could move another step Rudjek shot up to his feet and shouted. Mundo gave a running translation from a vantage point in the rear of the group.

"Klaido!" Rudjek called. "Don't forget your place! These people are our guests and under my protection."

Klaido whirled to face the priest, a positively evil grin on his reptilian features.

"Old man," he said in the language of Kemet, "tell me not what to do. I am Klaido, Friend of the Pharaoh—"

"Khafre is dead," Rudjek interrupted flatly, "and the new pharaoh unchosen. Take care, least you find yourself stripped of rank."

Tchay smoothly interrupted. "There's no reason for this argument. Not at this time. You arrive early, unexpected but welcome. Later this will all be sorted out. Klaido, Friend of the Pharaoh, come, sit. Eat with us. Later is time enough for talk. And action."

Klaido shuddered, barely containing himself. "All right," he finally ground out between his sharp teeth. "For you, Tchay, Well-Beloved Friend of the Pharaoh, I sit. I eat."

He rumbled through the dining room and somehow managed to squeeze himself behind the main table.

"Bring food," Tchay ordered, "for the Friend of the Pharaoh!"

Servants brought in huge platters piled high with roasted sheep and goats, ducks and geese. A groaning pair of servants staggered in with an entire half of a cow still on the spit. All this was piled in front of Klaido, who tore at the food ravenously, chewing and gulping with great vigor.

Other servants served multiple courses to the other guests. There was fish, ducks, goat, and beef. There were honeyed pigeons stuffed with rice and dates sweetened with sugar cane. There was barley beer and wheaten bread of all shapes. And for Struth, who was strictly a vegetarian, there were chickpeas and lentils, pomegranates and sweet lemons, savory onions, green lettuce, and mouth-watering grapes.

It was a wonderful feast. Or it would have been, if not for Klaido snorting and tearing at his food, crunching bones like they were pretzels and staring at Aaron and the others like they were the next course on the menu.

THE MAKING OF A MUMMY

"The boat's sailing smoothly," Eckels said. "Don't rock it."

"Yesterday you were suspicious as all get out about this character," Aaron said. "Today you're acting like he's our pal."

Eckels drank from his pot of beer. It was brewed from barley, and was excellent. The Egyptians already had had a thousand or so years experience in brewing. "All I'm saying is that things seem all right. Let's not screw up by acting foolish."

"It's not foolish to find out what's happening around us," Jennifer said.

Mundo nodded. "That's right. Khafre's death is bound to confuse things for awhile. They haven't even buried him yet, let alone picked his successor. It's no wonder that everything's up in the air."

"This is a slow country," Eckels said. He waved his hand languorously. "It must be the climate . . . all this heat."

"What do you want?" Aaron asked. "To do absolutely nothing? To sit around and let Tchay work his plans—whatever they are? And he's up to something. I'm sure of that." He turned to Mundo for confirmation. "You told me that he was an ambitious man."

"Well," Mundo temporized, "I haven't been around him that much—"

"Spill it," Travis said bluntly.

"Well—okay. Khafre, the deceased pharaoh, has four sons. For various reasons none of them would be an ideal pharaoh at this time. One's too young, one's devoted to the priesthood, one's not well liked by the people, and one . . . well, he's just too stupid."

Aaron grunted. "And Tchay knows someone who'd be the perfect pharaoh."

Mundo nodded. "Himself. It's not unprecedented. Dynasties rise and fall. Tchay rules a powerful nome. His official rank is Nearest To The Pharaoh, which is about as high as you can get. He's also a Well-Beloved Friend, which is better than Friend To The Pharaoh, which Klaido is. Apparently Tchay was a good buddy of Khufu, Khafre's father." Mundo shook his head. "This isn't something we want to get involved with."

"I agree," Aaron said, "but we don't want events to steamroll along, catch us unaware, and squash us. Klaido, for example. What's his role in all this?"

Mundo shrugged. "I don't know. I wasn't lying when I said I haven't been around too many high officials."

"Look," Jennifer said, "Klaido modeled for the Sphinx's face. The Sphinx is part of the mortuary complex—"

"And," Peter said, "we know who's in charge of that."

"Rudjek," everyone said at once.

"Think he'll see us?" Peter asked.

"Maybe," Aaron said, "if we asked politely."

"He's bound to be busy with this funeral business," Eckels objected.

"Sure, but it's worth a try," Aaron said.

"Maybe he cares for Tchay as much as we do," Jennifer put in.

"Maybe," Aaron said. "No sense in all of us trooping in. Mundo will have to translate."

"You and Peter go," Jennifer said. "Let's keep Struth in the background as much as possible. Travis and I will watch Eckels, just to make sure he doesn't hatch a little plan of his own."

Eckels snorted, but Aaron nodded. Jennifer made sense.

"Okay by me. Peter?"

"Let's do it."

Inside the Valley Temple it was hot enough to make the devil sweat.

"The best thing we could ever do for these people," Peter said, "is invent air-conditioning."

Aaron, wiping sweat from his brow, nodded. "I'd settle for the invention of the ice cube." He looked around. The scene, as usual, was one of controlled chaos. "Something's going on," he said.

"Maybe it has to do with the arrival of our pal, Klaido," Peter offered.

"Maybe." Aaron turned to Mundo. "How do we find Rudjek?"

Mundo shrugged hairy shoulders. "Yell real loud?"

"I liked you better before you developed a sense of sarcasm," Aaron said.

Mundo pouted.

"That was a joke," Aaron explained.

"Oh. Not a very good one," Mundo said. He turned and spoke to a pair of passing priests. They listened, nodded, and responded with words and gestures. Mundo looked smug. "This way," he said. "What *would* you do without me? No—don't answer that."

Rudjek was in one of the temple's inner rooms, sipping fruit juice and looking sour. Mundo apologized for barging in, but Rudjek waved it away. He seemed to be a priest who rarely stood on ceremony.

"Never mind," he said. "I wanted to talk with you all privately, but I've been busy." He sighed gustily. "There's some things I must supervise. If you care to come along, we can chat while I get some work done."

Mundo explained the situation to Peter and Aaron, and they nodded.

"What's he have to do?" Aaron asked.

"Oh," Rudjek said through Mundo, "check on how the mummy wrapping is going."

Peter and Aaron looked at each other.

"This should be good," Peter said.

The Valley Temple was a large building constructed of red granite. It was airy and spacious, though humming with the controlled chaos that was the hallmark of the entire mortuary complex. Rudjek led them to a small, windowless chamber that was occupied by half a dozen priests, several onlookers, and, of course, Khafre himself.

The priests looked up when Rudjek and the others entered, offered greetings, and returned to their work. Rudjek went to the onlookers and offered obeisance on one knee. He lingered to talk with them and Aaron and the others watched the priests of Osiris at their work.

Two were wrapping Khafre's corpse while the third supervised and intoned prayers. The body had already been wrapped in several layers of linen. The scent of perfume was heavy, but it couldn't quite mask the sweet-smelling, sickly odor of decay. Not unexpected, Aaron thought, considering the circumstances.

"That's, um, Khafre?" Aaron asked.

"Yep," Mundo said. "he's gone to his *ka.*"

"What's that mean?" Peter asked.

"It's a euphemism for croaking," Mundo explained. "The *ka* is like an astral body. It accompanies the physical body all through its life, and lives on when the physical body dies. It lives in the tomb. The Egyptians feed it and perform ceremonies in its name every day. Without a proper tomb the *ka* will wander endlessly and eventually shrivel up. Without food or remembrance it will also eventually cease to exist."

"How do you know this stuff?" Peter asked.

"Well, I asked, didn't I?" Mundo said. "These are a very friendly people. They're happy to discuss things with you if you're interested. Besides, I must admit that the concept of death is fascinating. It was never something I had to think about before."

"Looks like it takes a while to make a mummy," Aaron commented.

"Months," Mundo said. "First they wash and purify the body, of course. Then they prepare the head, removing the brains through the nose using this special hook—"

Aaron grimaced. "Spare the details, will you?"

"You sure?" Mundo said. "They're fascinating."

"I'm sure," Aaron said. "Just hit the high points."

Mundo shrugged. "If that's what you want. Anyway, once the head is prepared, they open up the body cavity and take out most of the internal organs. Have to. That's where decay first sets in. Once the organs—except for the heart and kidneys—are removed, they clean the body cavity, purify it, and pack it with wads of linen. Then they put it in a natron bath for forty days."

"Natron?"

"It's a chemical salt that absorbs moisture and is also an antiseptic. After the natron bath, the body's cleaned and purified and perfumed and is ready for wrapping."

"Like here."

"Like here," Mundo agreed. "The wrapping takes two weeks. Looks like they've already been at it awhile. As you can see, the wrapping is accompanied by hymns, incantations, and rituals."

"What're they doing now?" Aaron asked.

"The senior priest is putting amulets in strategic places among the wrappings. They're to protect parts of the body for eternity."

"When do they finally get around to burying him?" Peter asked.

"That's another fascinating question—" Mundo began, but Rudjek approached them before he could elaborate.

"We have to talk," Rudjek said. "But first excuse me while I say my prayers for he who has gone to the West."

Rudjek turned to the table and Aaron raised an eyebrow at Mundo.

"Right," Mundo said. "Another euphemism for death. The Egyptians always bury their dead on the west bank of the Nile, the direction of the setting sun."

The prayers didn't last long. When he was finished Rudjek motioned Aaron and the others, as well as those who'd been watching the wrapping process. Two of the onlookers were a middle-aged woman and a small, grave-faced boy who appeared to be her son. The third was also a woman. She was quite beautiful, but there was something different about her, something that didn't quite fit in with the others. As Aaron pondered this, Rudjek led them all to a sitting room away from the wrapping chamber. He seated the women solicitously, and turned to Aaron, Peter, and Mundo.

"This is Queen Persenti," he said, presenting the older woman, "and her son, the Royal Prince Menkaure. And this is Chantico, Khafre's favorite concubine."

Chantico. Of course. That's why she looked out of place. She was the woman Aaron had promised Tezozomoc he'd help return to the Aztec world. Looking at her, Aaron could see why Tezozomoc and Khafre had both loved her. She was beautiful in a wild, fiery way. She was dark-haired and dark-eyed like the Egyptians, but her features had a decided exotic cast with high cheekbones and a blade of a nose. Her hair was long and straight, her obsidian-dark eyes full of frank speculation as she regarded the newcomers.

"You going to tell her about Tezozomoc?" Peter asked.

"Tezozomoc?" she said quickly.

Smart, too. At least she had sharp ears.

"Um, yes. You'd better break it to her, Mundo. Gently, though."

"I'll try," Mundo said, and switched to Nahuatl, the Aztec language. Chantico listened with an attentive half-frown. She replied in the same language.

"What'd she say?" Aaron asked.

Mundo shook his head. "You humans never fail to amaze me. She knew in her heart, she said, that Tezozomoc was dead. He's been dead to her ever since she'd crossed over to this world. She's been here for years now, and she'd made herself another life."

"Pharaoh's concubine," Peter said.

Mundo scratched his head. "Apparently Khafre had quite a thing for artifacts—and visitors—from other time paths. It was sort of an obsession with him. He was delighted with Klaido, whom he eventually raised to the rank of Friend of the Pharaoh. You can imagine how pleased he must have been with Chantico."

"Hmmm," Peter said. "Who could blame him?"

Mundo grinned slyly. "Cool down, lover boy. Of course, she kind of thinks you're cute. Must be the red hair."

"Really?" Peter said, half-blushing, half-smiling. "Well—"

"Let's worry about your social life later," Aaron said. "We've got something more important to discuss."

"Yeah," Mundo agreed. "Like, what do we do about Klaido before he does something to us?"

Rudjek grunted at the sound of the Gairk's name, and Mundo questioned him. They fell into a long dialogue, Mundo ignoring the increasingly insistent questions from Aaron and Peter. Finally the ape sighed, nodded at Rudjek, and turned to face the others.

"Okay. Here's the story. Khafre wasn't exactly well beloved, but I guess he wasn't too bad for an oriental despot. Klaido did have his ear, and you know that Klaido's not exactly our friend. Oddly enough Klaido's got his own followers in the pharaoh's court. Of course, Khafre's dead, and that's the problem. Menkaure, there," he said, gesturing at the solemn child who was watching them with adultlike gravity, "is the best bet to succeed his father. But there's a problem."

"Kid looks like he's eight years old," Peter said.

"Exactly. Normally that doesn't present too much of a difficulty. A regent takes over for a couple of years—in this case say Queen Persenti, or maybe even High Priest Rudjek. I gotta say," Mundo lowered his voice conspiratorially, "this sounds suspicious to me, but apparently they're quite sincere. Unless they're really, really devious and can mask their thoughts well, I'd say they're both loyal to the kid. They simply want to hold the throne until he's big enough to sit on it himself. Others however, aren't quite so unselfishly loyal to the old dynasty."

"Tchay," Aaron said flatly.

"Tchay," Mundo agreed.

"I knew it," Aaron said. "He wants to muscle in and become the first pharaoh of a new dynasty."

"Exactly," Mundo said. "Now, if it was up to me I'd let these people sort out their own little problems.

However, it seems that Tchay and Klaido are best buddies. If Tchay gets the throne," Mundo paused dramatically and drew a finger across his hairy throat, "so much for our chances of getting out of here alive."

"So," Peter said, "we should help Menkaure hang onto the throne."

"Right."

Aaron nodded slowly. "I can see that. One question, though: what the heck can we do?"

"Well—" Mundo began, and was interrupted by one of the younger priests who came running into the room with less than priestly dignity, screaming at the top of his lungs.

"Simoooooonnn! Simoooooonnn!"

"What now?" Aaron complained.

Peter shook his head. "I don't know, but it sure as heck doesn't look good."

It didn't. Everyone else in the room looked terrified.

SIMOON

The air was hot and drowsy. Travis was supposed to keep an eye on Eckels, but he'd been through a lot in the past couple of weeks. He was wounded and tired and needed rest. Settled on a comfortable couch, a jar of barley beer in his hand, his head soon nodded, and he drowsed.

Eckels watched him sourly. He grunted when the guide drifted off to sleep.

"Great," Eckels said quietly. He rose, snuck past Travis, and headed outdoors. The sun speared him in the eyes and he threw up a hand to shade them. "Now what do I do?" he asked himself.

Tchay, he thought, seemed like a man he could deal with. Unfortunately they didn't speak the same language. Not even close. And the monkey was off jabbering with the old priest. Eckels was sure that he could cut a deal with Tchay, if he could only talk with the man.

He wandered the streets of the village, thinking desperately, distracted by the heat and the dust. What a filthy place, he thought. I've got to find the roadway that leads out of here. He had no desire to tackle the desert again, even if he could get the piece of temporal mechanism away from Aaron. There had to be another bit of roadway. If only he could find where . . .

A pair of men wearing short kilts and tight-fitting skull caps approached. Eckels turned his shoulders to let them brush past, but they didn't. They stopped in front of him. One had a badly scarred face, his left eye an unseeing milky ball. The other had bad teeth. He grinned and tapped Eckels in the chest with his stone-headed mace.

"What?" Eckels asked, irritated.

He gestured that Eckels should accompany them. Eckels sighed. He recognized a snatch when he saw one.

"All right," he said. "Take me to your leader."

The ways of the humans never failed to surprise, intrigue, and sometimes even instruct SStragh. Her irresistible impulse on meeting an avowed enemy like Klaido would have been to fight him to the death. That certainly had been Klaido's idea. The fact that he'd restrained himself seemed to prove that he was changing. He was straying from the OColihi, the Ancient Path that governed every aspect of their behavior. He was adapting. And, SStragh thought, if a Gairk could adapt, so could a Mutata.

SStragh looked around. Not that such adaptation was easy. She missed the ancient forests of her hometime. She missed the succulent plants growing everywhere. She even missed the companionship of other Mutata, though she had always been an outsider because of her reputation as a free-thinker.

Here was nothing but sun and sand and humans. The food was good, but strange. The climate was much too hot. She had to be careful to keep from overheating. She'd come very close to broiling in her own skin when they'd first entered this timeline. The humans were, well, human. Strange and unpredictable.

She looked at the young female sitting at her side. Even Jhenini was strange and unpredictable. Perhaps even more so than the others. SStragh couldn't define the feelings that she felt when she looked at Jhenini. There was no word in the Mutata vocabulary for friend.

"This is really amazing, isn't it?" Jhenini said. She had mastered the Mutata language as well as any human could. SStragh could understand her almost perfectly, even though she couldn't make the sounds the Mutata did through their nasal passages, nor could she consciously change her scent to give depth and nuance to her words.

"It is hot. I wish to go home," SStragh replied.

Jhenini laughed. It was a mark of the increasing bond between them that SStragh understood such complex human gestures without Jhenini explaining them. That thought made SStragh feel unaccountably content. Her crest rose and lowered quickly and she gave off the scent of tart citrus.

"I guess this is all very strange to you. To me, it's part of history. Even if it is a little twisted. It's fascinating to—say, isn't that Pawero?"

It was. The small human was industriously climbing through the shifting sand to reach the top of the dune where SStragh and Jhenini sat. He realized they'd noticed him and he stopped and waved, then his short legs pumped effortfully as he climbed the dune to reach them.

"Hello." Jhenini spoke the human word of greeting.

He answered her, though neither SStragh nor Jhenini could understand his words. SStragh knew enough about human expressions—though this one's face was obscured by the fur that covered the lower part of it—

to tell that he was concerned, or worried about something. He kept looking back over his shoulder.

"What does he want?" SStragh asked.

Jhenini shrugged. She didn't know. "I wish one of us besides Mundo spoke the language."

The short human stopped talking. He went down the dune a few steps, stopped, turned to them again, and gestured with his hands.

"He wants us to follow him," Jhenini finally said. "Maybe something happened to Aaron or Peter."

"If it has, it is as the All Ancestor wills."

Jhenini showed her teeth. It was, SStragh knew, a smile. That was still one of the gestures she was trying to figure out. It seemed to mean many, many things.

"Maybe. But did you ever think that the All Ancestor might want us to go and if we see can help them?"

SStragh thought about it. "That may be. Let us go."

Jhenini rubbed her neck. Her small, scaleless hand felt smooth and cool on SStragh's leathery hide. "Right. Let us go."

They followed the short human down the slope of the sand dune.

Jennifer touched Pawero on the arm and the dwarf looked up and smiled at her. He had a round, kind face. His eyes were dark and surprisingly intelligent.

"I wish that we could talk," she said, "and you could tell us where you're taking us."

He smiled enigmatically. Jennifer wondered, not for the first time, if they should trust him, but, she decided, sometimes you just have to trust people. If it came down to it, she'd much rather put her trust in Pawero than, say, Tchay.

They reached the village of craftsmen who were building Khafre's pyramid and mortuary complex. It was near midday and the streets were deserted. The

Egyptians followed a custom common in many warm-weather climates and took a siesta during the hottest part of the day. It seemed like a good idea to Jennifer. It was almost too hot to move.

Pawero looked around as they went down the street, as if he were keeping an eye out for someone. Once he must have spotted something suspicious because he pulled them into a side street and made them hide behind a mudbrick wall. Jennifer peered through a small crack in the wall and saw two men coming down the street. One had a badly scarred face and a dead eye. When the men had passed, Pawero urged them out of hiding and quickly took them down a small side street.

Jennifer recognized the building. It was Rudjek's estate, where they'd been taken the first night they'd come to the village. They entered through the front gate. Pawero gestured for them to wait and he scurried inside.

Struth looked down at her. Jennifer could see puzzlement and slight resentment in the way she held her body. "What in the name of the All Ancestor is happening?"

Jennifer shook her head. "I don't know. But I don't feel threatened. We should just go along—as long as it seems safe."

Struth lifted her head in agreement, stopped, and suddenly sniffed the air. "I smell rain."

"You do?" Jennifer asked. She looked at the sky. It was clear. "I'll bet rain's pretty uncommon around here."

Before Struth could reply Pawero returned and was gesturing for them to follow. They entered the manor house. It was cool inside. Jennifer glanced back before the door closed and saw what looked like clouds smudging the horizon. Black clouds.

"It does look like rain," she said.

* * *

"Why's everyone running around like chickens without heads?" Peter demanded.

Mundo shook his head. "I can't get any clear readings . . . it seems that the predominant thought in everyone's mind is dust . . . dust and fear."

Rudjek disappeared with his fellow priest after a hasty word of leave-taking. Chantico and Queen Persenti bundled the Royal Prince off somewhere deeper into the temple. Aaron, Peter, and Mundo were left alone and somewhat bewildered.

"Maybe we'd better go find the others," Aaron suggested.

"Good idea," Peter replied. "Let's go."

The Valley Temple was so deserted that they made it to the entrance without seeing anyone. Aaron stopped suddenly in the doorway and Peter ran into him.

"What's wrong?" Peter asked.

Aaron wandered outdoors, looking about wonderingly. "The air," he said. "Can you feel it?"

Peter stopped, frowned, and then put a hand out as if trying to touch something invisible. "It's cool . . . the temperature must have dropped ten degrees."

"Eighteen," Mundo corrected. "And I can taste water in the air."

"In this desert?" Peter asked.

Mundo nodded. "And it's not river water, either. It's fresh water, from the sky."

"Look!" Aaron pointed up.

"My lord . . ." Peter said.

They saw the first real cloud since their arrival in Kemet. They'd noticed some wispy things before, fluttering fragments that didn't deserve the name cloud. But this one did. It was huge, filling half the sky from the horizon to the deepest heavens. It was black as the most bitter night, black as the most evil soul. And it was coming towards them on winds that grew stronger and colder by the moment.

"What's that?" Aaron asked. "In front of the cloud?"

It was a changing shape, a brown amorphous mass that skittered on the ground and metamorphosed into a myriad of dark, frightening things before their eyes.

"It's dust," Mundo said flatly. "It's a dust storm."

A bolt of lightning emblazoned his words, a crash of thunder added an exclamation point.

"Run," Mundo screamed, and they did.

They panicked. They could have gone back into the temple and ridden out the storm with those inside, but the simoon touched something primitive in their minds. Unreasoning fear paralyzed the higher functions of their brains and their legs took over. They ran out into the open and tried to climb the hill of Khafre's pyramid and join their comrades on the other side.

They made it halfway up the hill and then the dust was on them, swirling like grainy fog so that they couldn't see, choking them like mummy wrappings so that they couldn't breathe.

A semblance of intelligence returned to Aaron. He grabbed Peter's kilt and Mundo's hairy back. He wound his fingers tight and screamed, "Stay together!" as he choked on a mouthful of sand.

The wind roared around them like unleashed tigers. Aaron felt Peter grab his own arm and Mundo buried his face in Aaron's back. He could feel the ape-creature whimper, but couldn't hear him. The wind snatched at them, pushing like a wrestler trying to topple them to the mat. Aaron leaned against it. He had the irrational thought that if the three of them weren't holding each other they'd be picked up by the wind and flung about like kites in a maelstrom. Then the wind howled harder and louder and Aaron decided that maybe the thought wasn't so irrational after all.

Lightning flashed and thunder crashed right on top of them. Just when Aaron thought it couldn't get any worse it did. The black thunderhead above them opened up and water ran like a river from the wounded sky.

Aaron cast about frantically, his eyes narrowed to slits against the driving wind, sand, and rain. Lightning struck not twenty yards from them, fusing sand into glass and illuminating a bizarre scene that could have come only from a fever dream.

A battle was taking place right before their eyes. Men wearing the ragged uniforms of the Confederacy marched across an open, sunny field. Some of them seemed to realize that something terribly strange was happening. Most were too intent on the blue-clad lines across the field to realize that their patch of world had been snatched away by fluxing temporal currents.

Aaron opened his mouth to shout but a noise louder and harsher than a hundred thunderstorms battered his ears as a volley of cannon fire devastated the Confederate ranks. Men were broken, twisted, and flung into the air like rag dolls. Aaron couldn't hear their screams over the horrible noise of thunder and cannon. He never saw if they completed their charge or were hammered into the earth by the Union artillery. They vanished as suddenly as they'd appeared, leaving another scene in their place.

A herd of dark, hump-backed animals thundered right at them. It took Aaron a millisecond to realize that they were buffalo and the sound he heard was the thundering of their hooves, not the thundering of the heavens. His mouth opened in astonishment as he saw among the wild rush of berserk animals a pair of horsemen guiding their ponies by knee pressure alone. They wore breechcloths and leggings. Their chests were bare but for painted designs. Their faces were those of American Indians. Their long hair whipping in the wind was decorated with feather rosettes. The rifles they held were unlike any rifles Aaron had ever seen. The front rider shot the herd's leader with a burst of laser light and the herd turned.

The Indian screamed exultantly, holding his rifle high. For a moment his eyes locked with Aaron's and he waved his rifle. Aaron lifted his hand, grinning weakly, and then the Indians and the buffalo vanished back into history, leaving a few of the outriding animals wandering around the sand with slightly glazed expressions.

It stopped as suddenly as it began. The windstorm washed past them; the timestorm burnt out. It took Aaron a moment to remember to breathe again.

"I thought we were goners," Peter said in a husky voice. "First the wind, then the cannons, then the buffalo . . ."

Mundo shook himself all over, shedding water like a dog. "I never want to go through *that* again."

"I'm with you."

The simoon had blown to the east, across and beyond the Nile where it was still a dark stain against the blue of the Egyptian sky. Aaron fell to his knees. He looked around, shaking his head. Twenty or so buffalo wandered around the hill of Khafre's pyramid. Most looked as stunned as Aaron felt.

"Boy," Peter said, "buffalo in Egypt. That's really going to mess things up."

"Not as much," Mundo said, "as that."

"What?"

Aaron looked where he pointed. A body wearing a Confederate uniform was lying facedown on the sand.

The earth around him was stained deep brown with his life's blood. A rifle was still clutched in his hand.

"Let's get the rifle," Peter said. He started forward, but Aaron grabbed his arm.

"Wait a minute. What for?"

"Why, so we can use it," Peter said. "For self-protection only, of course."

Aaron shook his head. "Think about it. What good would it do, even if there were thirty or forty cartridges with it?"

Peter thought about it. "Well, we're not going to conquer the world with it, but it *might* prove useful."

"It'll probably be confiscated by Tchay. We'd be better off if we just let it remain one of life's little mysteries for Tchay and his cronies."

"Hmmm. Maybe," Peter said. "Maybe you're right. What do you think, Mundo?"

The ape looked intently from Peter to Aaron. "If we keep quiet about it for now, maybe later, when we need it—"

"*If* we ever need it," Aaron corrected.

"Sure. *If* we ever need it, then maybe we can grab it."

"Okay," Aaron said. "It'll be our secret."

"Okay," Peter said.

They looked at Mundo.

"Oh, sure, okay."

Aaron knew that it was a gamble to trust Mundo, but there wasn't much else they could do. He looked around. The Egyptians were already coming out from shelter, staring at the buffalo who had appeared on Pyramid Hill. For the most part the buffalo stared right back.

TREACHERY

Travis was pacing the floor angrily when Aaron, Peter, and Mundo returned. The three were still wet from their unexpected drenching. Mundo's fur smelled a little musty.

"What's the matter?" Aaron asked when he saw the agitated expression on Travis's face.

"That no good son of a—"

"Eckels," Aaron interrupted. "What's he up to?"

"He's gone," Travis said flatly. "Gone. Vanished. Disappeared. Jennifer and Struth went out to get some air and I, I guess I dozed for a bit. When I woke up, Eckels was gone."

Aaron held his hands up placatingly. "Okay. That's not so bad. What can he get into? He doesn't speak the language, doesn't have any weapons, doesn't have any idea—" Something clicked in Aaron's mind. "Wait a minute—Jen and Struth. Where are they?"

"Well, they're gone, too. I saw the storm, figured I'd wait on you guys before I ran around aimlessly looking for Eckels. I figure they found shelter from the rain and wind."

"Let's hope so," Aaron said.

"I'm sure they're safe. What could happen to them?"

Aaron shook his head. "Plenty. Tell Travis what we learned from Rudjek."

Mundo filled Travis in with Peter supplying details. Travis shook his head when they were done.

"I think we'd be better off if we avoided getting caught in the middle of this."

"We do too," Aaron said. "But we might not have a choice. Remember, Klaido wants us dead. If his faction gets into power, we might as well start building our own little pyramids. We'd need them pretty quickly."

"No doubt about that," Peter put in glumly.

"Another thing," Aaron said, looking thoughtful. "When that thunderstorm rolled through it was accompanied by a timestorm."

"Anything interesting happen?" Travis asked.

Aaron thought about the gun and their pact to keep its existence a secret. He figured it wouldn't really hurt to let Travis in on it, but he'd tell the guide later. Now there were more important things to occupy their attention.

"The usual weird stuff. But here's something I've just realized. Haven't you noticed that most storms—certainly the most intense ones—all have something in common."

"Yeah," Peter said, "they all scare the heck out of you."

Aaron grinned. "Besides that."

Travis rubbed his chin thoughtfully. "Now that you mention it, yeah, there is something. Most occur near Floating Stones—pieces of the temporal roadway."

"Exactly," Aaron said. "Maybe not all of the storms hit near the roadway, but most of them do. Especially the intense ones."

"And this one was *intense*," Mundo said with a shiver. "The thought of that buffalo herd coming right for us still makes my fur stand on end."

"Buffalo herd?" Travis asked.

Aaron waved a hand. "We'll go into that later."

Peter frowned. "Well, that's a great theory, except for one problem. *I* didn't see any Floating Stone near the pyramid."

Aaron nodded again. "Nope. But how about *in* the pyramid?"

"I think you've got something there," Travis said excitedly. "What are pyramids for? Storing treasure, right?"

They all nodded.

"And what did Khafre value above everything else? Artifacts from the different timelines, right?"

They all nodded again.

"And what better artifact—"

"—than a piece of temporal roadway," Aaron said with some satisfaction. "It's got to be there, in the burial chamber, waiting for Khafre's mummy. We've got to check it out. We've got to find that bit of highway and see where it leads. It could take any of us home."

"Yeah, but going inside the pyramid?" Peter asked.

Aaron remembered that his friend suffered from claustrophobia. He'd already had his fill of enclosed, dark places when he'd had to climb through a tiny fissure in the heart of a hill to escape a pair of Gairk hunters on the Dinosaur World.

"It'd be too conspicuous if we all went." Aaron thought for a moment. "Travis, you and Peter go look for Eckels—and it wouldn't hurt to keep an eye out for Jen and Struth. You're probably right; they're probably okay, but I want to know for sure."

Travis nodded decisively. "Right. Then you and Mundo are going to explore the pyramid's interior?"

"If we can get in. I'll need Mundo to do the talking if we have to get past any guards."

Mundo nodded. "Anything that'll bring me closer to home. Anything."

Despite the urgency of their situation, Aaron and Mundo stopped for a moment and watched the astonished Egyptians round up the buffalo that had appeared so suddenly in their midst.

The buffalo herd mentality had held fast. The first thing they did when confronted by the Egyptians was gather together in a tight knot. They seemed dazed and confused, Aaron thought. He sympathized. He knew the feeling well.

But he was glad they were there. They provided the diversion he and Mundo needed to get into the pyramid. Even the two men guarding the entrance had run off to join the roundup.

"Let's go," Aaron said. "Nobody's looking."

He and Mundo approached the pyramid, glanced around, and ducked inside the lower entrance. There was a second doorway in the wall, but it would have taken a climb of some thirty feet up the side of the pyramid to reach it. Aaron was sure they'd be spotted if they tried to use the upper entrance.

Inside the entranceway it was dark and cool. There were hand torches and a guttering lamp to light them with. Aaron lit one of the torches and passed it to Mundo, started to light another, then stopped.

"I just had a thought," he said. "Suppose some workmen are still inside, finishing up the last-minute bits and pieces."

"Leave them to me," Mundo said confidently.

Aaron nodded, keeping his doubts to himself. "Okay," he said. "Here we go."

The passageway was made of unfinished stone blocks with rough, unpainted surfaces. It was maybe five feet high and four feet wide. Aaron was glad that he wasn't claustrophobic like Peter. The corridor sloped downward at a rather precipitous angle, but the unfaced stone floor provided a fair grip for their feet. Once inside Aaron had to stoop uncomfortably. Mundo was Aaron's height but he was used to walking slightly scrunched over.

After a descent of a hundred feet or so, the passageway suddenly leveled for a stretch, then began to ascend. They went up almost as far as they'd gone down—and going up was tougher on their leg muscles than descending. The air was close and still and it was hot inside the passageway, even by Egyptian standards. Aaron felt sweat pouring down his back and trickling down his forehead into his eyes. At last they came to another level stretch, and their torches showed that the tunnel branched.

One arm of the corridor went upward and back in the direction they'd just come from.

"That must be the way to the upper entrance," Aaron said in a low voice, his whispered words bouncing eerily off the stone passageway.

Mundo agreed. "We must go the other way," he said, pointing to the branch that ran in the direction they'd been traveling.

Aaron agreed. The passageway was still narrow and cramped, but at least it stayed level, easing the cramps in his aching leg muscles.

After another fifty feet or so, the passageway finally opened up and Aaron could stand upright. He sighed and swiveled his neck around. The chamber at the end of the passageway was small, but at least they could stand erect in it. It was dark, its corners untouched by the guttering light thrown by their primitive torches. Aaron's last-minute fears proved groundless. There were no workmen inside. The chamber looked empty.

"Khafre's burial chamber," Aaron said, and Mundo nodded. "Not much to see, but let's make sure."

The two started a slow circuit around the room in opposite directions, flushing out the darkness from the chamber's corners and edges. After a moment Aaron smiled in satisfaction.

"There it is," Aaron said softly. Mundo came and stood by him. "Our ticket out of here."

A bit of temporal roadway drifted inches above the stone surface of the chamber's floor.

"This must have been the crown jewel of Khafre's collection," Aaron said. "Besides Klaido, of course. I guess he wanted it buried with him."

Mundo nodded. "Shall we try it?" he asked eagerly.

Aaron shook his head. "Better not. We don't want to get separated from the others, especially if there's a time differential between this world and wherever that one leads."

"Maybe home," Mundo said wistfully.

"Maybe," Aaron said. "For some of us."

Home. It had never seemed so far away. Aaron wished he could walk into downtown Green Town, order a double burger, large fries, and chocolate shake at Mac's Drive-In, then go home to his own bed, collapse, and sleep for a week. He was tired. More and more he felt responsibility weighing him down. He wondered how it had all fallen on him. He hadn't asked for it. Maybe, he thought, you never do. Maybe it just comes to you as you discover that you're the one who has to run things, the one who makes promises to save others, like Chantico, or fix things, like he'd vowed when he learned of the death of his Grandpa Carl. Aaron had never really thought of himself as a leader, but maybe leadership was something that you didn't think about. Maybe it just came to those who could lead, whether they wanted it or not.

"Um, Aaron?" Mundo said questioningly, pulling him out of his reverie.

"Yeah?"

"Over there. There's a light."

Aaron frowned, turned, and squinted back at the chamber's entrance. Mundo was right. There was a light. Aaron fought a sudden sinking feeling as he stared into it, trying to discern who held it. It looked almost like a child.

The light came closer, and Aaron suddenly realized that the torch was held by Tchay's fool, the dwarf Pawero. The dwarf smiled as he came into the chamber. Aaron's sudden fear turned to puzzlement and then rapidly turned back to fear again as he saw the two men who followed Pawero into the burial chamber. They were armed with spears and they weren't smiling.

Not at all.

Eckels frowned in disgust as he paced around the room in which he'd been unceremoniously tossed. He was getting very tired of this whole thing. What he needed was a gun and a couple of ammo clips. Then he'd show these savages who was boss. It wasn't much to ask for. But no, that adolescent fool Cofield had decreed that they'd leave all their technology locked in the time machine back on the lizard's world. The idiot.

There was a sudden sound at the chamber's door as the bolt was thrown and the door opened wide. Outside was the scar-faced man who'd brought Eckels to this place. He smiled, and it made him look even more sinister.

"Where's your friend with the bad teeth?" Eckels asked in a pleasant voice.

His kidnapper scowled and gestured with his stone-headed mace.

"Okay, I get the point, Ugly," Eckels said. "You want

me to come along." He smiled sweetly and nodded. "You know, I've dealt with lizards prettier than you. At least they'd make a nice pair of boots if you skinned them. You're just too damn ugly to be worth anything."

The scar-faced man gestured down the hall. Eckels preceded him, out of patter for the moment. He lapsed into a brooding silence, trying to come up with a plan that would put him back in control. It didn't improve his outlook when he couldn't think of anything.

The corridor opened into a big room, a tall-ceilinged hall that might have served as an audience chamber. At least that's what Eckels figured it was.

Tchay sat in an ornately inlaid golden chair that looked beautiful, but very uncomfortable. It didn't seem to bother him, though. He sat ramrod straight and stared at Eckels as he entered the chamber. It was a good thing that the hall had tall ceilings, because Klaido stood to the right of Tchay's throne.

"Oh-oh," Eckels said.

Struth was big and impressive; Klaido was bigger and terrifying. Klaido's ancestors had been carnivorous, and so was he. Nearly ten feet tall, his body was almost ponderous with muscle but Eckels knew that the lizard could move like a pursuing monster in a bad dream. His eyes were cold and reptilian. Eckels had to constantly remind himself that the brain behind them was as good as his own. Well, perhaps not *his* own, but certainly as good as the average human's. Klaido's mouth was huge and grinning, showing teeth like daggers. He smelled like death and he reminded Eckels uncomfortably of the Tyrannosaurus Rex he had tried, and failed, to stand up to.

Klaido stared at him. Eckels couldn't meet his hideous glare for long. He dropped his eyes to Tchay and noticed for the first time what lay across the nomarch's lap.

"Well . . ." The smile crept back on Eckels's lips. "There is a god."

It was a rifle. Eckels couldn't see any details from where he was standing, but it was a rifle of some kind, all right. He wondered how it had gotten into Tchay's hands, then dismissed the question from his mind. Since he'd gotten involved in the unraveling timelines he'd seen many stranger things.

Tchay gestured for him to approach, and he did. He stopped a few feet in front of the nomarch and bowed low.

"Greetings, oh mighty would-be king. What do you have there?"

Tchay glanced at Klaido and spoke in his ancient tongue. Klaido seemed to understand. He answered, after a fashion, in what could have been the same language as interpreted by a Gairk's vocal apparatus. There were a lot of roars and grunts and squeals, but Tchay seemed satisfied with the lizard's answer.

Klaido gestured with one of his forelimbs. It looked almost dainty compared to the rest of him, but Eckels knew that that three-clawed paw could eviscerate him with one swipe.

"I see," he said. "You've picked up a gun somewhere and you want me to take a look at it? You remember, don't you, you miserable lizard, what one of these things can do? Only problem is you're too stupid to figure out how it works."

The three looked at each other for a long moment, Eckels assessing the situation. Finally, when Tchay thrust the rifle at him, Eckels nodded and smiled broadly.

"Sure, you miserable savage. I'll show you how it works. Then maybe you could so something for me, hmmm?"

They seemed to understand each other even though

they spoke different languages. Eckels took the rifle. He looked at it, frowning. It was an ancient piece. In Eckels's hometime it would have been in a museum with the relics of other ancient epochs. But it was a gun, and Eckels was experienced with guns. He looked at it for a moment, then nodded.

"What we have here is a single-shot muzzle loading rifle." He looked down the inside of the barrel, squinting. "Probably originally a smooth-bore percussion musket, its barrel was later rifled to—" He looked up to a couple of blank stares. "Oh, never mind. This is what you want to know."

He grabbed the rifle by the stock. "You put the cartridge in here," he said, indicating the open mouth of the barrel. "You did get cartridges to go with this thing, didn't you? Otherwise, you might as well just forget shooting it and use it as a club."

Klaido and Tchay looked at each other. For the first time Eckels noted the resemblance between the two, particularly in the eyes. Tchay held up a leather pouch that had been sitting by the side of his chair.

Now, Eckels thought, here comes the delicate part. He actually wasn't sure about all this stuff, but now wasn't the time to be hesitant.

The pouch contained, as he thought it would, cartridges encased in paper. He wasn't sure if you had to rip the paper, or what. He thought he would err on the side of caution and do as little to the equipment as possible.

He took a cartridge and put it down the muzzle. He tamped it in with the rod that had been stored under the barrel. The cartridge pouch also contained a handful of percussion caps. He took one out, showed it to Tchay and Klaido, and put it in place. The cap was struck by a little thingamajig called the hammer when the trigger was pulled. The hammer crushed the cap's copper head, igniting a small bit of powder. The tiny explosion traveled down the rifle's vent, igniting the cartridge and firing the gun. Simple. But by no means as efficient or devastating as the modern weapons locked up in the time machine back on the Dinosaur World.

Eckels decided not to demonstrate the rifle himself. Klaido was leaning forward, staring like a cat before a mouse hole and Eckels knew that he was the rodent in question. One false move and Klaido'd snap his head off like a lollipop off a stick.

Eckels held the rifle out, careful to keep his hands far away from the trigger. He offered it to Tchay, who got up hesitantly and took it. Eckels mimed the proper shooting position and Tchay awkwardly followed suit.

"Excuse me, kingy. It's like this."

He approached Tchay, and placed the nomarch's hands in the proper place, braced the butt of the rifle against Tchay's shoulder. He crooked his own trigger finger.

"Now do that."

Tchay looked doubtful, but did as he was told. The resulting explosion was as immense as the billowing clouds of black smoke that issued from the rifle's barrel. Eckels could tell that Tchay liked neither the smoke, the noise, nor the kick of the weapon, but he was mightily pleased when he saw the hole the bullet had gouged in his plaster-covered wall. He took the butt from his shoulder and actually smiled. Eckels smiled back and returned the cartridge pouch. There were about ten cartridges in the pouch, along with a handful the percussion caps.

"There you go," Eckels said. "Have yourself a grand time." He rubbed his chin thoughtfully. "And now," he added, "let's figure out what you can do for me."

* * *

There was a freshness in the village that Travis and Peter had never felt before. It was as if the cloudburst had revived everything, like the sudden and unexpected arrival of spring. Naked children splashed through the few puddles that still remained, romping with equally muddy village dogs. There was a coolness to the air, a sweetness that would soon evaporate like the puddles themselves, but nevertheless made them feel more alive than they'd been feeling for quite a while.

"I know," Peter said after a minute, "that we're supposed to be looking for Jennifer and Struth—"

"And Eckels," Travis interrupted.

"And Eckels. But just how do we do this? We can't go around knocking on doors."

Travis scratched his head. "Struth should be easy to spot. The others, though . . ." He let his voice trail off. "Maybe we'd be better off not finding Eckels."

Peter was silent, but he sort of agreed. He knew that he'd fallen in with Eckels a couple of times when he should have stayed out of the man's machinations. Several times Eckels's schemes had endangered the whole group, not to mention the time that he'd abandoned Peter to the tender mercies of the Gairk. Still, he was one of them. They couldn't just abandon him. Could they?

Peter was mulling this over when they suddenly found themselves face to face with a nearly naked, wiry-muscled man carrying a stone-headed mace. He planted himself imperiously in front of them and motioned for them to stop. Peter noticed right away that the man had really bad teeth.

"What now?" Peter complained aloud.

Travis studied the intruder. "From the looks of his gestures I'd say that he wants us to come with him."

"Oh, he does, does he?" Peter flamed with sudden,

nearly irrational anger. "Well, I don't think I want to go with him. I don't like his looks."

"Easy, son. This could be trouble."

"Trouble?" Peter asked. He'd suddenly had it. He was tired of running, tired of the hopeless feeling that came with the realization that they weren't in control of their lives. "Trouble? Let me tell you about trouble. Ever since this thing started there's been nothing but trouble. I've been chased by intelligent carnivorous dinosaurs. *That* was trouble. I was captured by intelligent herbivorous dinosaurs, then I was captured by Indians who tried to sacrifice me to their buzzard cult. *That* was trouble. I've been shot at, had spears thrown at me, tied up, jumped off thousand-foot-high vertical cliffs using a stuffed pterosaur as a hang-glider. Heck, I had to live for weeks in a cave with Eckels as my only companion and rat stew the only thing to eat. And *I* had to catch and skin the rats. *That* was trouble.

"*This* is only a small, ugly guy with really bad teeth and a club."

Peter reached out suddenly and grabbed the club. The man looked at Peter with an astonished expression. Peter turned, twisted, and heaved, and the man went flying over Peter's shoulder. He let go of his mace and hit the ground heavily. He looked at up Peter with fear in his eyes.

"And now *I've* got the club."

Peter stared at the man, who scrambled to his feet and went off in a limping run.

"There," Peter said with satisfaction. "So much for trouble."

Travis shook his head. "I don't know if that was wise."

"I'm tired of being wise. I want to kick some butt."

Travis looked up the street. "Maybe you'll get your chance."

Peter looked where he pointed. The man with the bad teeth stood at the end of the street. Six or seven others were with him, similarly dressed, similarly armed. They looked at Travis and Peter. They didn't seem happy.

"What do we do now?" Travis asked.

"Run," Peter said without hesitation.

"Good idea."

The two turned and ran down the street, the mob in hot pursuit.

SECRETS REVEALED

"I don't think," Mundo said cautiously, "that they mean us harm. The guards are angry that we snuck in while they were chasing the buffalo, but Pawero is calming them down."

The jester succeeded in this with much capering and clowning, face-making and cajoling. At last he had the guardsmen laughing and they put up their spears. Pawero then turned to Aaron and Mundo and spoke rapidly and urgently.

"He says to come with him," Mundo translated. "He says that Jennifer and Struth are under his protection."

Aaron looked dubious. "What kind of protection can a court jester offer?"

Mundo shook his head. "I don't know. But there may be more to the guy than there seems. He's got the mind of someone who has a lot of secrets. When I try to probe it I mainly see smoke and mirrors."

"Well, I guess we've seen what we came to see. I don't suppose it could hurt to follow Pawero's lead."

They followed the dwarf and the soldiers out of the pyramid. The sun was so bright that it hurt their eyes, though it was good to get into the open and breathe fresh air again.

The guards took their customary positions at the pyramid's lower entrance and Mundo and Aaron followed Pawero as he led them down the hill.

"Ask him where he's taking us," Aaron requested.

"To the village," was Mundo's translated reply.

They went through the town by way of back alleys and little-used streets. Aaron got the impression that they were trying to avoid someone. He considered asking Mundo to press Pawero about it, but then decided to let things take their course. He would, however, remain alert to danger and be ready to react to anything.

Only there was nothing to react to. It was as peaceful and carefree as a stroll through the park. On the outskirts of the village they reached a walled manor that looked familiar. Pawero knocked on the closed gate. A square peephole slid open and a face peered at them for a moment. Then the peephole door slid shut and the gate swung wide open. Pawero gestured for them to enter.

Inside was the manor house the travelers had been brought to the first night they'd arrived in Kemet. Rudjek's house. Aaron had never been there before, but Mundo had told him all about it. It was mainly one story, flat-roofed, and built from mudbricks that had been painted a dazzling white. Behind the house rose three tall conical buildings that looked like gigantic beehives. Aaron guessed they were granaries. There were a couple of other outbuildings of a more problematical nature. Off to one side, half hidden behind the main house, was a small lake surrounded by flower beds and fruit trees. Struth was sunning herself by the lakeside. Jennifer was tossing crumbs to a horde of quacking ducks.

"Jen!" Aaron shouted.

She heard him, looked up, and ran towards them.

She flung herself into Aaron's arms and they hugged fiercely.

"I was worried about you," Aaron said.

"You should know by now that I can take care of myself," Jennifer told him. "Besides, Pawero's been a wonderful host."

"Yes," Aaron looked down at the dwarf, who was beaming up at him and Jennifer. "I wish I could figure out what his game is."

"I know," Mundo said smugly.

Aaron turned to him. "You know? Why didn't you say anything?"

"I just figured it out," Mundo protested, "on the walk over. It was the first opportunity I had to spend some time near Pawero and probe a little more deeply."

"So?" Jennifer and Aaron said at the same time.

Mundo smiled. "He's a secret agent."

"What?" Aaron asked.

Mundo nodded his head. "Incredible, isn't it? All this time we thought he was just a goofy court jester. Well, he's an agent of the pharaoh's court. He was 'given' to Tchay some time ago to keep an eye on him. It seems that we're not the only ones suspicious of the nomarch."

"Is this true?" Aaron asked.

"Of course it is," Mundo replied in aggrieved tones. "You doubt me?"

Aaron shook his head. "It's just . . . just hard to credit. He's . . ."

Aaron's voice ran down. He was about to say, "He's just a dwarf," but he realized how narrow-minded and unfeeling that sounded.

"I guess I should know not to judge anyone by their appearance," he said.

"Yes, you should," Mundo said, puffed up with self-righteousness. "After all, looking at me you'd think I was just a monkey."

"Ape," Jennifer corrected. "But what exactly does Pawero want with us?"

"I'll ask," Mundo said. He spoke with Pawero for a few moments, nodded, then turned to Jennifer and Aaron. "He wants us to come inside for lunch. Struth too."

Jennifer and Aaron looked at each other. "Okay," they said.

Eckels was steamed, but there was little he could do about it.

Tchay's men thrust him into the cell, closed the door, and slammed the bolt home. He jumped to the cell door and grabbed the bars on the door's tiny window. He shook them angrily, but they were well set in the solid wood door.

"Last time I help you with anything!" he shouted after Tchay's men, then he jumped back as Klaido suddenly thrust his face against the small window.

The dinosaur seemed to grin at Eckels. Drool dripped off his long, sharp fangs. You didn't have to read his mind to know that Klaido didn't have Eckels's welfare foremost in his thoughts. His long red tongue licked his lips and fangs. Eckels thought he looked hungry.

"You're not going to have me for lunch," Eckels said. He sounded more pathetic than brave.

After a moment Klaido went away and all Eckels could do was sit on the floor, his arms wrapped around his knees, and hope that his fellow time-travelers would come looking for him.

It was more luck than superior endurance that enabled Travis and Peter to outrun their pursuers. They ducked down one of the twisting, mazelike alleys, and soon found themselves so lost that they had no idea where they were. The man with the bad teeth and his henchmen had long vanished. Their only problem lay in extricating themselves from the village without running into their pursuers again.

"What do we do now?" Peter asked. They stopped to catch their breath under a brightly-striped awning. A small, naked child looked up at them with big, dark eyes. Peter smiled at the kid as sincerely as he could.

Travis shook his head. "We're in a fix. We're in the middle of something big. I'm not exactly sure what."

"Nobody is," Peter said sourly as the child ran off into a nearby mudbrick dwelling. Peter looked up to see what the child had been staring at. He took a deep breath. "But I think things just got a little more complicated."

"Damn," Travis said. "They're on to us."

Peter shook his head. "It's not them. It's someone else. Someone I've seen before. He's one of Rudjek's priests."

The man was dressed in priestly garments, but he was also armed and grim-looking. It was no wonder that the child had run away. He was accompanied by another figure, smaller, and wrapped in a cloak and robe that must have been stifling.

The priest stopped before Peter and Travis and made a gesture of obeisance. Looking relieved, he started to chatter in the ancient Kemet language.

"Wish I knew what he wanted," Peter said.

Travis pursed his lips thoughtfully. "I think he wants us to come with him. The question is, should we?"

Peter shook his head. "Not unless we figure out what he wants with us and where he's going to take us."

The cloaked figure suddenly let her hood down. "Peter?"

Peter stared. "It's Chantico—the girl from the Aztec world. Right?"

She nodded, pointed at herself. "Chantico."

She took Peter's arm and tugged gently. Her expression was concerned, almost urgent.

"Maybe," Peter said, "we'd better go with them."

"Just a minute!" Travis protested. "One second you don't trust them, the next you want to go traipsing along."

"Yeah, well," Peter said slowly, "that was before I knew she was involved."

"You trust her? Why? Because she's fluttering those long eyelashes at you?"

Peter looked away from her, to Travis. "Well—no. Not really. We can trust her. She's with Rudjek's faction. Rudjek is a nice guy. At least he seems to be."

Travis sighed with exasperation. "Oh, sure. He *seems* like a nice guy."

"Look, we're never going to discover anything if we keep wandering around at random. We've got to take some chances and I think this chance is a good one to take. I'm going with her."

Chantico was following the conversation eagerly, seemingly understanding the gist of it. She smiled when Peter finished speaking, and ran her hand through his red hair. She patted his cheek, then pulled him after her speaking urgently.

"I think she wants us to be careful," Peter said.

Travis sighed again. "Yeah, you think. All right. I guess I better tag along. Just to keep you out of trouble."

"Too late for that," Peter said.

FUNERAL FOR A PHARAOH

"Basically," Mundo said after a delicious lunch, "Pawero tells me that at first he didn't know what to make of us. He was suspicious because we all came from another timeline, like Klaido. He thought we were Klaido's friends, friends who planned to back him and Tchay in the struggle after Khafre's burial."

"Why's Klaido siding with Tchay?" Aaron asked. "He and Khafre were friends, after all."

Mundo questioned Pawero, but it was evident from the agent's shrug and uncertain expression that he didn't understand the Gairk's motives.

"He doesn't know," Mundo said. "I might hazard a guess. Khafre was apparently strong—perhaps autocratic. Tchay is much the same way. The Gairk are used to strong leaders, someone who tells them exactly what to do and when to do it. There's no such candidate among Khafre's legal successors. So, to Klaido's thinking, why not Tchay? He'd certainly be strong enough. Besides, perhaps he made Klaido promises, maybe a promise to send him home, though I guess that's as improbable as us finding our own way home.

"The thing is, Pawero eavesdropped on some meetings between Tchay and Klaido. He knows that we and Klaido are enemies, that Klaido wants us all dead."

"At least," Jennifer said, "we have mutual enemies."

"That's right," Mundo said. "So we have a basis for working together."

"What's he want from us?" Aaron asked.

"He wants us to get rid of Klaido. To take him home if we can. Just, I guess, to dump him somewhere if we can't."

"He could have him killed," Aaron pointed out.

Mundo nodded. "He can. And he will if he has to. But he'd rather take Klaido out of the picture another way. It's something religious to him. A concept of not doing bad in this life so nothing bad will happen to him in the next. He'll have Klaido killed if he has to, but he'd rather not take on the burden of bad deeds."

"Interesting," Jennifer said. "That sounds like the Buddhist idea of karma. If you do something bad it'll come back to haunt you in a later life."

"I'm not worried about a later life," Mundo said. "Right now I'm pretty much concerned about how this one is going to end up."

"You're not the only one," Aaron said. "When will Khafre's funeral begin?"

"Well," Mundo said, putting on his best professorial air, "strictly speaking, it's already begun. The mortuary rituals start with the preparation of the body and end with its interment inside the pyramid."

"Which will be?" Aaron prompted.

"Tomorrow, actually."

"When does Pawero suspect Tchay will act?"

"Pretty much as soon as Khafre's mummy is out of sight."

Aaron groaned. "That gives us plenty of time to figure out some kind of plan." He stopped and looked around. "Say, has anybody seen Peter or Travis lately?"

Everybody exchanged glances and shrugs.

"Maybe they're with Eckels," Mundo suggested.

"Let's hope they're safe," Jennifer said.

"No," Peter said. "No, not another. Please . . ."

Chantico, reclining on the lounge next to him, offered him another honeyed date, a pouting smile on her beautiful features.

"I think she likes you," Travis said, sipping his jar of barley beer on an adjacent lounge.

"Well it's about time I got some kind of break in this traveling through the universe business." He turned his attention back to Chantico. He couldn't help but smile. "Well, all right. Maybe just one more."

Her smile broadened and she popped the date into his mouth. He chewed languorously. They smiled dreamily at each other.

"Listen," Travis said, "I hate to break up your date and all, but don't you think we'd better try to find Eckels?"

"Forget Eckels," Peter said. He reached for the goblet that Chantico offered, his hand lingering on hers as he took it from her grasp. He took a sip. It was diluted wine, sweetened with honey. It tasted a lot better than the harsh barley beer that Travis favored. He took another sip, then handed it back to Chantico. She turned the cup so that her lips touched the rim where Peter's had and drank from it herself.

"Um, Travis. Why don't you go tell the others that we can't find Eckels?"

The guide drained his jar of beer, put it down and stood. "Two reasons, mate. First, I get the impression from the way Chantico brought us here that it's not safe to walk around the village. Second, because we haven't really looked for Eckels yet, which we're going to as soon as you stop playing kissy-face with the Queen of Sheba there."

Peter sighed. "I suppose you're right." He sat up and took Chantico by her shoulders. For a second, touching her soft, satiny skin almost made him lose his train of thought. But he took a deep breath and, looking straight into her deep, dark eyes, said earnestly, "Eckels? Do you know where Eckels is?"

She listened attentively. She nodded and gracefully slid off the lounge. Kneeling on the floor she bowed her head and lifted her arms, crossing them at the wrist.

"She's acting like she's a prisoner or something," Travis said.

Peter nodded. "Chantico." She looked back at him. He crossed his own wrists. "Eckels?" he said again in a questioning tone.

She nodded.

"By who? Where?" Peter asked.

"Let me guess," Travis said in a grim voice. "Tchay."

Chantico turned at the sound of the nomarch's name, looked at Travis, and nodded.

"That's just great," Peter said. "Do we try to break him out?"

"We weren't supposed to get involved in local politics," Travis said. "Now we're going to have to save Eckels's worthless hide."

"How do we do that?" Peter asked.

Travis shook his head. "You got me, son."

The day of the pharaoh's funeral dawned cool and clear, like every day in Kemet. Aaron, Jennifer, Mundo, and Struth assembled on the west bank of the Nile along with a multitude of others, waiting for the ceremony to begin. They were worried. Peter and Travis—not to mention Eckels—were still missing. Pawero had taken off to see if he could discover their whereabouts, but he'd told the time-travelers that he couldn't spare much time or effort tracking down their missing comrades.

Pawero was sure that Tchay would try to grab the throne today, probably after Khafre's mummy was placed in the pyramid. Because the nomarch would have his mind on these weightier matters, Pawero was pretty sure that they were all safe from Klaido—for now.

"Besides," Pawero had told them before disappearing into the crowd, "Tchay's agents would never dare attack you in this multitude."

It was an impressive gathering. The elite from the pharaoh's court at Mennufer had come down the Nile for the ceremony, along with all the important provincial officials, the nomarchs and their retinues, priests from every important temple and cult in the land, merchants, aristocrats, soldiers, scribes, and diplomats and ambassadors from the cities, provinces, and kingdoms of near Asia.

The time-travelers blended into this disparate crowd nicely. Even Struth elicited few comments, though some of the provincial officials and diplomats had never seen her like before. They marveled at her appearance and obvious intelligence.

The crowd was quiet and respectful, but still there was the buzz of dozens of conversations as the onlookers waited for the funeral to begin. Suddenly, a loud, eerie wailing, a heartbreaking keen of grief and sorrow, came from the Valley Temple and the crowd fell utterly silent.

"This is it," Mundo said. "It's beginning."

A group of women came from the Valley Temple. They were dressed in dull blue-gray cloaks smeared with dust and mud. Their faces, contorted into hideous masks of grief, were also dirt-streaked. Their hair was long and wild and as they advanced from the temple they pulled at it, wept loudly, and cried in terrible sorrow.

"Is that the pharaoh's family?" Jennifer asked. "His wives?"

Mundo shook his head. "Nope. They're pros."

"Pros?" Aaron asked.

"Professional mourners. And since this is the pharaoh's funeral those are the best that money can buy."

They watched silently as the weeping mourners led the procession into the early morning. Following the mourners were three columns of servants, arranged twenty deep. They carried a variety of items. Some carried flower arrangements ("Apparently some things haven't changed," Aaron muttered to Jennifer), others bore trays with offerings. There were jars of oils, some to be be burned in lamps, others soothing, perfumed potions for the skin. Some of the offerings were food: dates and figs and fruit of every description, whole baked fishes and salted meats and several varieties of fresh baked bread. Other servants carried boxes of clothing and personal items like combs, jewelry, sandals, and other items that had been Khafre's favorite geegaws.

"There it is," Aaron whispered, pointing. "Look!"

It was the piece of temporal roadway. They'd removed it from the burial chamber where it'd been under guard so it could be interred formally with the pharaoh's other favorite possessions. Two servants were carrying it as it hovered slightly above a flat wooden platform they'd hoisted on their shoulders.

"Our ticket out of here," Mundo said. "Only question is, where will it take us?"

Jennifer shook her head. "Maybe home, Mundo."

"Yeah, maybe. Maybe not."

"You never used to be such a pessimist," Aaron said.

"That was before I met you guys," Mundo retorted. "Look, here come the *shabtis.*"

Following the servants bearing the offerings and Khafre's personal possessions was another group with trays of small statues ranging in size from a few inches to over a foot in height. There were literally hundreds of the things. Aaron and the others were close enough to the procession so they could see that the little statues all looked similar—Aaron supposed that they were depictions of Khafre himself—but they were all in different poses, doing different things.

"What're all those—what's you call them?"

"*Shabtis,*" Mundo supplied.

"Right. What are all those *shabtis* for?"

"Well," Mundo said, obviously enjoying his opportunity to show off his superior knowledge, "the Egyptians think life after death is pretty much like life before death. There's plenty of work to do. But if you have these little statues in your tomb, you can send them to take your place. You can relax and enjoy your afterlife while they do all your work for you."

Aaron nodded. "Makes sense, I guess."

Jennifer suddenly clutched his arm. "Will you take a look at that?" she said.

"Ah," Mundo said. "Looks like the guest of honor has finally arrived."

A boat, maybe twenty feet long with a mast almost as tall, suddenly hove into view. It seemed to be sailing on the sand. It took a moment before the entire ship came into sight and Aaron and the others realized that it was actually resting on a wooden sled being pulled with ropes by scores of servants. On the deck was a mummy-shaped sarcophagus. Inside the sarcophagus was Khafre's mummy.

Preceding the vessel, the mortuary boat as Mundo called it, was a battalion of priests. Rudjek was in the lead. He wore a black panther-skin cape, his traditional long white linen robes, and a serious expression. A number of priests were dressed like Rudjek, but apparently there were other types of priests who wore different kinds of animal skins, ostrich-feather headdresses, and robes of a different cut.

After Khafre's mortuary vessel came his family, led by his wives and children.

"Someone's missing," Aaron said, frowning. "Chantico isn't among the mourners."

"That's odd," Jennifer said.

"She's probably up to something," Mundo said with a frown.

"Don't be so suspicious—" Jennifer started, but Struth interrupted her with a nasal blatt that expressed warning and anger.

"Klaido!" the Mutata hissed.

Klaido was among the next group of mourners, following Khafre's immediate family. He towered above the humans, looking more like a misplaced circus animal than part of a funeral procession.

"Ah," Mundo said, "maybe we should, ah—"

"Pawero said we'd be safe," Aaron said firmly.

Klaido's beady eyes picked Struth out of the crowd. He opened his mouth, hissing, and exposed row upon row of sharp, evil-looking teeth, but the Gairk was too much a creature of habit, ceremony, and tradition to interrupt the funeral of his pharaoh.

"I don't like the look he gave us," Mundo said.

"Pawero was right," Aaron said. "We'd better watch ourselves once the funeral is over."

"Look at Tchay," Jennifer said. "He's got a gun of some sort."

He was among the dignitaries following Khafre's immediate family and he was carrying a rifle by the barrel like a walking stick. His expression was hard and stony, but there was something smug in it that made Aaron feel very uneasy. His three wives were with him and a passel of kids that Aaron guessed were his children.

He and Mundo looked at each other. "It's the rifle that came through the timestorm," Aaron said.

"What?" Jennifer asked.

"I'll explain later," Aaron replied. "Think he knows how it works?"

"Hard to say," Mundo said. "I can't get a deep reading on him, but he seems sort of smug. And he really seems to be anticipating something. Anticipating it with great eagerness."

The court dignitaries brought up the end of the procession, but the onlookers joined the tail end of the line as it headed up the hill to Khafre's pyramid.

"Oh-oh," Aaron said. "I just thought of something."

"What?" Jennifer and Mundo asked in unison.

"Well, if the temporal roadway is going to be put in the pyramid with Khafre's mummy, and then, if the entrance to the pyramid is sealed—"

"How are we going to use it to leave Kemet?" Jennifer finished for him.

Aaron nodded. "Exactly."

"Okay," Mundo said. "Here's what we do. We create a distraction of some kind, a diversion. It should be easy. Then we jump on the roadway now. It'll take only a few seconds—"

"Good idea," Aaron interrupted. "I've got the pieces of temporal machinery." He patted the small sack slung over his shoulder. "But what about Peter and Travis?"

"And Eckels," Jennifer put in. "We can't forget Eckels."

"No," Mundo said sourly. "I guess we can't do that, can we?"

* * *

Eckels had stopped pacing around his tiny cell. It was getting him nowhere but tired. He sank down in a corner of the room with his back against the wall and grumbled to himself. He grumbled about everything, about how hot it was, about how hungry he was, about how it was everyone else's fault but his own that he was stuck alone, hot, and hungry in this little room. He added Tchay's name to the list of people he'd get even with when given a chance.

He slept fitfully. He was too hungry and uncomfortable to sleep well. He looked up hopefully when the door to his cell opened, but something told him that it was bad news when the man with the dead eye stuck his head inside the room.

He smiled evilly and gestured for Eckels to get up.

"All right, you ugly little jerk," Eckels said with mock cheerfulness. "I hope you're letting me go, or at least taking me to breakfast."

The man with one eye grabbed Eckels by the arm and pulled him into the hallway. Eckels might have taken a chance and jumped him, but he wasn't alone. Three other men were with him. All were armed with stone maces or sharp-pointed javelins, so Eckels thought it best to go along with whatever they wanted.

What they wanted was to march Eckels down the corridor. For once he kept quiet. He suspected that he was in trouble—even more trouble than usual—so it surprised him when they led him out of Tchay's house.

"They're letting me go," he said to himself, and even managed to smile at his captors.

But instead of taking him to the front gate, they marched around the back to where a deep pit was dug next to the wall that enclosed Tchay's estate. Whatever was in the pit smelled old and musty and rotten and Eckels didn't like it one bit.

"Wait a minute!" Eckels protested as they marched him to the pit's edge.

The man with one eye gestured and Eckels craned his neck to see what was in the hole. Looking up at him was the largest crocodile Eckels had ever seen. It opened its mouth and hissed. It looked hungry.

The man with one eye said something that made everyone—except Eckels, of course—laugh. Then two of the men grabbed Eckels by the arms.

He fought back but he knew that it was too late.

PANDEMONIUM

Something touched Peter on the face, waking him. He jerked back and shot out a hand which encircled a slender, cool-feeling wrist. Chantico leaned over the edge of his bed with a low laugh. She said something. Peter couldn't understand what she said, but he smiled back.

"We've got to learn each other's language," he said.

"Eckels," she said.

Peter sat up. "You've found Eckels? You know where he is?"

Chantico nodded. The disturbance finally roused Travis, who was sleeping across the small chamber from Peter.

"What is it?"

"I think Chantico found Eckels. She wants us to go with her."

"Give me a minute," Travis said, wearily rubbing his face.

They took more than a minute. Chantico went from the room as the two dressed and returned with fruit juice, freshly baked bread, and cold meat for breakfast. They ate hurriedly. The sun was rising as they left the Mortuary Temple where Chantico, with the help of Rudjek's priests, had hidden them for the night.

They went straight for the village, which seemed quiet and deserted, even for this time of day. People rose early in Kemet, while it was relatively cool. But this morning they saw few people, and all of them were scurrying toward the Nile.

"Something must be going on," Travis said.

"Yeah, and we weren't invited."

They stopped at one of the walled estates near the center of the village. Chantico led them around the back, away from the main street and also from the front gate. She motioned with her hands as if she wanted Travis and Peter to lift her up.

"I think she wants a boost," Peter said.

He put his hands on her slim waist and she smiled and said something. Peter wished he knew what it was. He lifted her up. Travis helped steady her as she put her hands against the wall. She pushed against Peter's chest with her bare feet and grabbed the top of the wall. She looked over for a moment, then dropped down silently to the ground. After another moment the gate opened and she motioned for them both to come in.

Inside the wall was a large manor house, some outbuildings, and palm and fruit trees. It was like Rudjek's estate, but on a larger, more lavish scale.

"I wonder who owns this?" Travis asked quietly.

"I don't know, but I hope they've gone off with everyone else in town."

Chantico put her finger to her lips, shushing them with the universal sign for quiet. They started toward the villa, but a sudden, loud voice stopped them.

"Wait a minute!"

Peter and Travis looked at each other.

"I'd recognize that voice anywhere," Travis said.

Peter nodded. "Eckels. And it sounds like he's in trouble. We'd better hurry."

They dashed around the house. Eckels was definitely

in trouble. Two men holding his arms were about to toss him into a big pit while two others watched, laughing and apparently offering advice.

Peter quickly outraced Chantico and Travis. He ran as hard and as quietly as he could. The men were making so much noise and were so intent on dumping Eckels that they didn't hear Peter until he was right on top of them.

Peter smiled. He felt like he was back on the gridiron. One of the men turned just as Peter reached him, lowered his shoulder, and hit him full speed with a nice blind-side block.

The man yelled and smashed into one of the men holding Eckels. He staggered and teetered at the edge of the pit, windmilling his arms desperately to regain his balance. Eckels put his foot on the man's backside and pushed.

He screamed all the way down.

One of the men let go of Eckels and grabbed for his companion, missing him by a scant inch. Eckels booted him in the butt and he, too, went screaming over the edge. The other man tried to push Eckels after his comrade, but Eckels pulled free with a strength born of desperation.

Without feeling too bad Peter clubbed the Egyptian down from behind with a blow to the back of his neck. He fell to his knees, clutching his head and moaning. Eckels kicked him viciously in the ribs.

That left the one-eyed man.

"Hey!" Peter said. "I know you!"

Apparently the man also remembered Peter. He took one look at him and ran away by Travis and Chantico, who were just arriving on the scene.

"What the heck is going on?" Travis asked, then the screaming started in the pit below.

Peter, Travis, and Chantico peered over the edge of the pit curiously. Peter quickly looked away.

"There's a big alligator down there eating those men!" he exclaimed.

"Crocodile," Travis corrected automatically.

"Good!" Eckels said savagely. "Let's give him some dessert."

He went to the man moaning on the edge of the pit and would have tipped him in, but Travis and Peter both stepped in front of him.

"You can't do that," Peter said.

"Why not? They were going to do it to me."

Travis shook his head. "Let's not argue about it. Let's just get out of here."

Eckels sniffed. "That's fine with me."

The four of them hurried back to the gate.

"Who are these guys, anyway?" Peter asked.

"Tchay's goons," Eckels replied. "He was going to feed me to the crocodile, even after I showed him how to work the gun."

"You what?" Peter asked.

"What gun?" Travis asked.

"The rifle. It must have come through the time-storm."

"You showed Tchay how to use it?" Peter asked, unbelievingly.

"Well," Eckels said judiciously. "I had to, didn't I?"

"I'll bet," Peter muttered.

They were out in the alley that ran by the back of the estate. Chantico shut the gate behind them.

"We'll straighten this out later," Travis said. "Question is, what do we do now?"

"Hook up with the others," Peter said.

"Right." Travis looked at Chantico. "Think she can lead us to them?"

"I'll bet," Peter said. He turned to Chantico. "Aaron? Jennifer?"

Chantico smiled, nodded decisively, and led them back through the village toward the pyramid towering like a mountain over everything.

The procession stopped before the entrance to Khafre's pyramid. The funerary rituals began, Rudjek leading them. Mundo explained everything to the best of his understanding. It was interesting stuff, but Aaron was getting more and more worried as things progressed.

He wracked his brains to come up with a plan, but couldn't think of a thing.

"They're starting to put the offerings in the tomb," Mundo said.

"I know," Aaron said.

"What are we going to do if they seal the temporal roadway in the pyramid?" Mundo asked.

"I don't know," Aaron said.

Struth suddenly took a deep breath and let it out slowly through her nostrils. "A Dreaming Storm is on the air," she said to Jennifer in Mutata. "I can smell it."

Jennifer translated.

"What next?" Aaron asked.

"Say," Mundo said. "Look over there. Isn't that Peter and Travis and Eckels?"

"I wonder what's going on," Peter said. "I've never seen so many people gathered in one place at one time. The entire village must be here."

"More people than that," Travis said. "Look at the base of the pyramid. Something is happening by the entrance. Let's get a closer look."

They pushed through the crowd as politely as they

could, getting more than one angry murmur and glance.

"That's a coffin all right," Travis pronounced. "I think they called them sarcophagi here."

"They must be putting Khafre into the pyramid," Peter said.

"Think they put a lot of treasure in with him?" Eckels asked eagerly.

"Oh, shut up already," Travis said.

Peter turned to Chantico. "Khafre?" he asked, motioning towards the ceremony now taking place at the pyramid entrance. She nodded eagerly.

"Oh-oh," Travis said. "I think I recognize our one-eyed friend. And he's not alone."

Jennifer held a hand out, then looked up at the clear blue sky.

"I could swear that I felt a rain drop," she said. "But there's not a cloud in the sky."

The one-eyed man had rounded up a party of Tchay's henchmen who were among the crowd and they started toward Peter and the others. They didn't care who they pushed and jostled, but few protested when they saw the looks on their faces and the weapons they carried.

"What do we do now?" Peter asked.

Travis shook his head. "I don't know."

SStragh held her head high, sniffing the wind. The smell of the coming storm made her nervous. She'd been content to sit back and observe the strange human ceremony. She liked ritual. Strange as it was, it reminded her of home, and the endless, complicated, comforting ritual of the OColihi. But the OColihi, as comforting as it was, was leading her people down the path to extinction.

The human ceremony, too, if allowed to continue, would end with their imprisonment and probable death. She suddenly knew that she could not allow this to happen. She suddenly knew what she must do. She must stop the human ritual from ending.

She stepped forward, towering above all the humans around her, and screamed her challenge to Klaido.

"It's Struth!" Peter shouted, the Mutata's hideous cry drawing his—and everyone else's—attention to the intelligent reptile as she pushed through the crowd around the pyramid's entrance.

"There's Peter and Jennifer and Mundo!" Travis said.

"What are we waiting for?" Eckels cried. "Let's go to them."

SStragh heard Jhenini shout her name, but she ignored her human companion. She pushed to the front of the crowd. Klaido knew what she was doing and shoved through the humans around him until they met face to face in a cleared area before the pyramid entrance, every eye riveted on them.

"What are you doing, foolish Mutata?" Klaido roared in their language.

"What I should have done long ago," she responded. "Issuing the *ciosie,* the challenge to combat."

"Why?" Klaido asked.

"I will not allow you to kill my friends," SStragh said. There was no equivalent word in the dinosaur language, so she used the human word.

"They are as good as dead already," Klaido said. "And now so are you."

He advanced angrily.

* * *

"Aaron!" Peter called out. "Jennifer!"

Aaron heard him, turned, and waved vigorously. "Over here!" He grabbed Jennifer's arm. "Come on. It's Peter and Travis. They have Eckels and Chantico."

"We have to help Struth," Jennifer said.

"We will," Aaron promised. "Somehow. Right now let's just get together."

The two groups pushed through the crowd until they met.

"What—" Aaron began.

"Explanations later," Peter said. "Right now we've got to figure out something. Look!"

He pointed. The one-eyed man had rallied his cronies and they were closing in on the time-travelers.

"What'll we do?" Eckels asked.

A lightning bolt split the empty sky and the crowd moaned.

SStragh charged.

She and Klaido met tooth and claw in front of the pyramid as lightning tore the sky. They were unarmed but for the weapons nature had given them, fangs and talons powerful enough to rend any flesh. Klaido was bigger, obviously stronger. But SStragh was fast, agile, and determined.

She ducked as Klaido roared and fastened her teeth upon his throat. Her teeth were the flat, dull teeth of the herbivore, but her jaws were powerful. Klaido's roar turned to a scream of pain. He raked SStragh's neck with his sharp talons. Her hide was tough, but his talons were sharp. Blood sprang out on her neck, spurted where the cuts were deep.

She pushed with her powerful hind legs and Klaido fell, pulling away from her jaws. She spat, disgusted by the taste of flesh and blood.

* * *

"A timestorm is going to break soon," Jennifer said. "Don't you see? Someone is going to activate the temporal roadway."

"And that someone might as well be us," Aaron said. "Come on, let's go."

As they started to run toward the pyramid the sky turned black. It wasn't the black of night. It was more frightening, much more unnatural. It was the black of a sudden, unexplained eclipse, of a deep shadow cast by an eerie, unseen presence. The air smelled wet and strange. People in the crowd started to scream. And panic.

The one-eyed man's gang pursued the time-travelers, but there were still many people between them. Aaron thought for the first time that they could make it to the temporal roadway. He gave silent thanks for the note of caution that'd made him pack along the collection of temporal mechanisms.

They reached the pyramid's entrance as Rudjek and the other priests watched with astonishment.

"No time to explain," Aaron called to them, "even if I could."

Mundo reached the temporal roadway first. He hesitated, looked back. Aaron waved at him.

"Go on, go on! We can't afford to wait."

Mundo stepped on the roadway. The timestorm hit as he vanished.

There was no rain this time, just jagged lightning and awful thunder and the smell of ozone in the air. The timestream fractured like a geological fault in an earthquake. Strange scenes flickered into existence beside the pyramid and the crowd gathered for Khafre's funeral broke and ran. Khafre's family and the court dignitaries gathered by the pyramid entrance milled

DINOSAUR EMPIRE SKETCHBOOK

A Record of My Adventures
by Aaron Cofield

Pages 2 and 3: Mundo's fangs glittered prominently in the torchlight as the Egyptians confronted us.

Page 4: Bizarre enough that the face of the Sphinx was a dinosaur, but when I realized it was the head of the human-hating Klaido…

Page 5: Mundo in his now-traditional role of interpreter explaining the situation to Chantico in her native Nahuatl.

Page 6: Klaido and Tchay gleefully examine a weapon from another millennium.

Page 7: Their screams lasted the entire way down…

Pages 8 and 9: The beast that attacked Travis in the blizzard.

Pages 10 and 11: The peculiar procession of soldiers leading dinosaurs down the Appian Way towards Rome.

Page 12: Lucius' ego took a severe beating when he lost to an ape in oratory.

Page 13: Peter is outfitted for his new job as one of the Pretorian Guard.

Pages 14 and 15: The crowds cheer (and we all wince) as Klaido and Struth face each other in gladiatorial combat.

Page 16: We look back on Publius Servius' burning villa as we make our escape.

about uncertainly. Tchay stepped forward, his face flushed with anger.

"Watch out!" Aaron shouted. "He's aiming the rifle."

He leveled the weapon, but hesitated. He couldn't decide on his target. At the last minute he whirled and pointed the muzzle right at Menkaure, Khafre's youngest son and the one most likely to succeed him as pharaoh. Queen Persenti, Menkaure's mother, didn't know what the rifle was but she knew that Tchay meant her son harm. She flung herself in front of the boy. Before Tchay could pull the trigger, a cartwheeling dwarf appeared out of nowhere. Pawero smashed into Tchay, full speed.

Tchay lost his footing. He dropped the rifle and screamed as he slipped, fell, and rolled down the hill to where SStragh and Klaido were fighting.

Eckels jumped upon the roadway, followed quickly by Peter and Chantico, who were hand in hand.

Jennifer shouted at Struth, "Please, Struth, come with me, now! Please!"

Struth hesitated. Klaido was floundering, trying to get his footing in the loose sand stained with his blood. She had the choice of hurling herself on Klaido or going to her friend's side. She chose her friend.

"Come on, Aaron," Jennifer called over the rolling thunder.

"You go," Aaron said. "I have to go last."

Jennifer nodded. She knew there was no time to waste arguing. She and Struth went through together. Travis stopped to scoop up the rifle Tchay had dropped and took it with him as he vanished on the roadway.

That left Aaron and Klaido.

Aaron was tempted to leave Klaido, but he'd promised Pawero that he'd try to do something about the Gairk. What, he had no idea.

Klaido finally managed to get to his feet in the loose

sand. His eyes, Aaron thought, looked more insane than usual. The maddened dinosaur charged up the hill. Tchay, lying in his path, looked up as Klaido stepped on him and struck suddenly like an angry snake. Tchay didn't even have time to scream.

Aaron looked around. The crowd near the pyramid had dispersed in terror, though Pawero was still looking at him curiously.

"I wish I could explain this mess," Aaron said, gesturing helplessly, "but I can't. I've got to go before Klaido catches up to me. Take care of yourself—and your new pharaoh."

Aaron jumped onto the temporal roadway just as Klaido finished with Tchay. There was blood on his muzzle and madness in his eyes as he stomped up the hill of shifting sand, losing a step with every two that he took.

They locked eyes for a moment, then the nausea gripped Aaron and he knew he was going to a new world.

ANOTHER WORLD

The nausea was as nauseating as ever, the feeling of dislocation as dislocating. Aaron thought he'd never get used to those sensations no matter how many times he moved between worlds.

He appeared with the usual headache, sick stomach, and thudding heart. He closed his eyes for a moment to gather his thoughts and strength. It was dark, quiet, and pleasantly warm without being hot. He opened his eyes and looked around. For a moment he was afraid that he'd find himself alone again. This time he sighed with relief.

"All right," Peter said. "The gang's all here!"

And they were. Peter and Chantico, Travis, Eckels, Mundo, Jennifer, and Struth were crammed inside a dark building. It was night, so Aaron could discern few details as he glanced around. For a moment he was startled by several huge figures along the walls, but he relaxed when he realized they were only statues. The darkness had fooled him into believing they were alive. He sighed and grinned at Peter's welcoming words. Then he suddenly remembered the last thing he'd seen before leaving Kemet.

"Yeah, but I'm afraid the gang's going to get even bigger. Last thing I saw before leaving town was Klaido tearing Tchay to pieces and heading right for the temporal roadway."

"Well, deactivate it!" Eckels demanded.

Aaron hesitated. He'd promised Pawero that they'd try to do something about Klaido, but having the kill-crazed dinosaur show up in their midst didn't seem like a good idea. Maybe if they deactivated the roadway now they'd catch him suspended between worlds.

"I'm way ahead of you."

Aaron dropped to his hands and knees, and tugged at the piece of temporal mechanism embedded in the bottom of the floating roadway. It wouldn't come loose.

"It's stuck," Aaron said between gritted teeth.

Peter dropped down on his knees. "Let me help."

The position was awkward. Neither could use their full strength. The mechanism clung stubbornly no matter how hard Aaron and Peter tugged.

Aaron gave up after one last attempt.

"Forget it!" He jumped to his feet. "We've got to get out of here before Klaido shows up. We won't stand a chance against him if he catches us cooped up in here."

Struth understood most of what Aaron said.

"I have challenged him," she said in her hooting, nasal English. "I will finish our fight."

"Maybe," Aaron said. "But not in here."

"He's right, Struth," Jennifer said. "Please, let's get outside."

Struth bobbed her neck in agreement.

"The door's over here," Mundo said.

"You can always depend on Mundo to find the escape hatch," Travis said dryly.

Mundo led the way out into the night. They had to go down a dozen long, narrow stone steps that fronted the structure. It was apparent that the building was abandoned. Blown brush and fallen branches choked most of the stairway. The humans found it difficult and

Struth found it impossible to climb down without help. The fact that it was night didn't help. The sky was clear but moonless, warm, and dark. They were in a forest clearing and the trees surrounding them obscured the sky and stars.

"Any idea where we are?" Aaron asked.

Eckels was studying the building they'd just vacated. "You know—" he began, and was interrupted by a hideous roar that reverberated from the structure's interior like the scream of an enraged beast.

"Klaido!" Mundo shouted, eyeing the nearest tree.

Struth faced the building squarely. "I will deal with him," she said calmly, reverting to her native tongue and speaking in an almost ritualistic pattern.

"You don't have any weapons," Jennifer said, also speaking Mutata.

"Neither does he," Struth said reasonably. "It shall be as it was in the days of the Ancestors. Tooth and claw."

"He's bigger than you," Jennifer said. "He's stronger, and his teeth are sharper."

"What's going on?" Aaron asked.

Jennifer turned to him desperately. "Struth wants to fight Klaido hand to hand. She doesn't stand a chance without weapons."

"Good," Eckels said. "It'll give us a chance to get away."

"Eckels—" Travis began warningly, and then Klaido burst out of the building. He stopped at the top of the stairs, looked at the time-travelers, and screamed a loud, angry diatribe in Gairk. Of course, Gairk always sounded loud and angry. Still, it was apparent that he meant them no good.

Aaron was fresh out of plans. "Scatter!" he shouted. "Head for the trees!"

That way at least Klaido couldn't get them all.

Klaido roared a final spurt of hate and anger, started after them, and promptly fell, rolling heavily down the steps. Before he could regain his feet the timestorm hit.

It was the worst they had ever seen, the most sudden and the most savage.

There was no rain this time, but blowing snow that withered them with arctic cold. Vague shapes moved through the blizzard. At first Aaron thought they were doing some weird pattern-dance. Only when a pair of the shapes stumbled toward him did he realize that they were fighting to the death.

One was an apelike creature with long, thick, white fur. Its features were a grotesque parody of humanity's, with nothing cute or lovable about them. The other was even worse. There was nothing human about it, nothing suggesting life of a kind that Aaron had ever seen before. It was a collection of rods and spheres aligned in an alien symmetry, combined with tentacles and pseudopods that the creature seemed to grow at will.

It was trying to engulf the apelike being, who was fighting back desperately with a primitive stone hand-axe. The alien thing was winning. It had successfully engulfed an arm, leg, and most of the ape's back and shoulders. The ape caught Aaron's eye and Aaron was shocked to recognize the pain, intelligence, and pleading on its face. He took a step forward and then realized that he couldn't risk being swept into the creature's hometime. He watched helplessly as the tentacles of the alien being pulled the rest of the ape-creature into the embrace of its engulfing pseudopods.

The ape-creature screamed, then the liquid flesh of the alien being filled its mouth, choking it to silence. With the ape taken care of, the thing seemed to sense

Aaron for the first time and started to move toward him making sucking, squishing sounds.

Aaron retreated. He didn't want that thing any nearer. An icy hand clutched his shoulder from behind and for the first time he understood the meaning of the expression, "his heart jumped into his throat," because his seemed to do just that.

"It's me, Eckels," his fellow time-traveler said. Aaron could have kissed him in relief. "I'm freezing. Let's get away from this damn blizzard."

"And the things in it," Aaron said fervently.

Eckels cocked his head and looked at him closely. "Things?"

"You didn't see the, uh, things, in the snow?"

Eckels shook his head.

"Then you're lucky. Come on."

Aaron's words were punctuated by lightning that was bright enough to momentarily turn night into day. They staggered off together into the trees.

The storm seemed to go on and on. Among the trees they were free of the knife-edged wind and the blowing snow, but it was still bitterly cold. After the days spent in the warm sunshine of ancient Kemet Aaron felt frozen half to death. At least he and Eckels seemed relatively safe, but what about the others?

"Jennifer?" he called. "Peter? Travis?"

"Hey." Eckels put his hand on Aaron's shoulder again. "If there really were things in the snow, do you think it's wise to yell like that?"

Aaron shook him off. He was too cold, tired, and worried to argue.

"Struth?" he shouted. "Mundo?"

There was the crash of a falling body through interlocking tree branches and Mundo landed in a heap at Aaron's feet.

"Oooofff!" he said, and got up, dusting his pelt.

"Well, you finally got around to calling me. Last, as usual."

"Sorry, Mundo," Aaron said. "Have you seen the others?"

"Oh, sure. It's not, 'How are you, Mundo?,' 'Are you okay, Mundo?,' 'Did you manage to escape frostbite, Mundo?,' it's—"

Aaron sighed. "Okay, Mundo. How are you?"

Mundo looked aggravated. "How am I? I'm cold, that's how I am—"

"Fine, you're okay then," Aaron said. "Have you seen the others?"

"Maybe," Eckels interrupted, "they're over there."

"Huh?"

Aaron turned to look where he was pointing. Far away, barely visible through the forest, a small light was twinkling in the distance. It looked like a campfire, warm and inviting.

"That's where I'd be," Eckels said.

"Me, too," Mundo put in. "Let's go."

"Wait a minute," Aaron said.

The two stopped and looked at him. After a moment Eckels said, "Yes?"

"Well . . ." Aaron didn't want to leave the area without the others, but Eckels was right. The campfire burned like a beacon in the dark. The timestorm was subsiding, but it was still cold and wet. Their comrades could have been attracted by the campfire. Still—

"It might be dangerous," Aaron said. "After all, we don't know where we are. Or when."

Eckels looked at Mundo. "Listen to him. It *might* be dangerous," he said sarcastically. "When haven't we been in danger lately?"

He started to walk toward the campfire.

Mundo looked at Aaron. "I hate to say it, but I've got to agree with him. We have a better chance of finding the others there than we do standing around in the dark."

Aaron nodded. "You're right." He hated to admit it himself. "Let's go."

Eckels turned, waiting for them.

"But we stick together," Aaron said. "And we be careful."

"Absolutely," Eckels agreed.

"Certainly," Mundo said.

Aaron suppressed a sigh. He had a bad feeling about this.

The blizzard petrified SStragh. She had experienced nothing like this in her life. There were no words in her vocabulary for snow or ice. It seemed as if the sky were breaking into pieces and falling down on them. Beside the awful terror she felt, she had also never been so cold in all her life.

Klaido still lay in a heap by the stairs. He got up groggily as the pieces of sky cut at them, whipped by harsh winds that stole all the strength out of SStragh's limbs.

"Struth! Struth!"

It was Jhenini. No one else mangled her name quite like that. She honked in reply and a shadowy form approached through the blinding storm. It got quite close before SStragh recognized Jhenini. She was making an odd sound. SStragh finally realized that her teeth were clicking together quickly. The Mutata had never heard that sound come from a human before.

"It's so cold," Jhenini said.

SStragh wanted to reply, but suddenly couldn't think of what to say. The cold, she realized, was starting to affect her brain. Her kind wasn't built to take temperatures like this. Heat she could deal with, dissipating it through her skin, radiating it away through her nasal horn. Cold, though, was a killer. Her body couldn't manufacture its own warmth. Take the heat away from her surroundings and she'd slowly shut down. It was interesting in a way, because it had never happened to her before. Of course, it was also deadly, but somehow that realization didn't seem to matter too much.

Slowly SStragh sank to the ground, which was already covered by a carpet of cold, broken sky several inches thick.

"No!" Jhenini said loudly in the human language, but that didn't matter too much, either. SStragh was very tired. She thought that a nap would be nice.

Jhenini laid down next to her, snuggling close. Her body had the warmth of a banked fire. It was pleasant. SStragh blatted contentedly.

Close to the two, odd shapes moved in the storm.

Chantico had never seen snow before. At first, it rather enchanted her. Then she started to realize just how cold it was getting. She looked plaintively at Peter, rubbing her bare arms to get the circulation going.

Peter looked at Travis, who was standing next to him as Klaido came tumbling down the stairs. "If Klaido doesn't get us we're going to freeze our butts off."

Travis nodded and waved the rifle he'd brought from Kemet. "We have to get out of this wind and snow. Let's head off toward the trees. They'll act as a windbreak."

"We can't run off without the others," Peter said.

Travis shook his head. "We won't. We'll hang close, just out of the edge of the storm. It should break up soon. These things don't last long."

"Okay," Peter said.

He threw his arm around Chantico's shoulders and she snuggled close. She fit well and felt good there. She seemed to think so too because she smiled up at him despite the cold. He wished he had a shirt that he could give her, but of course they didn't wear shirts in Kemet. They didn't wear much of anything so no one was particularly prepared for the bad turn of weather.

"Hey," Travis suddenly said. "One of the others is coming toward us!"

Peter squinted against the stinging, wind-driven snow.

"I don't know," he said. "It doesn't look like—"

Chantico screamed.

It didn't look like anything Peter had ever seen before in real life or in nightmares. It sort of sucked up to them out of the snow. It was oddly built, jointed in a frighteningly alien way. Its body consisted of attached ovals of flesh. Its limbs were slightly slimmer, more fluid ovals. It was hard to say if it had a head or not, or if it wore clothes. It did have tentacles. There were so many of them and they were whipping about so rapidly, that Peter couldn't count them. They were all mesmerized, even Travis who had seen many strange and terrifying creatures in the timelines he'd visited as a safari guide.

Travis was the first to come to his senses.

"Get back!" he barked, as the thing moved towards them without moving.

It extruded a pseudopod of flesh, swiftly, silently, from the bottom of its body and engulfed Travis's legs from the knees down.

Travis screamed.

It was the most terrifying sound Peter had ever heard from a human throat. Peter froze as the thing shot out half a dozen ropelike tentacles that whipped around Travis and tried to draw him nearer. Peter stared, desperately wondering what to do, torn between running or trying somehow to save Travis. Acting more out of years of finely honed reflex than any conscious thought, Travis threw the rifle up to his shoulder. It was primed, ready to fire.

But the creature was just as fast as Travis. As the hunter cocked the rifle the thing shot out half a dozen tentacles, wrapping them around the gun barrel and stock. Travis yanked back and pulled the trigger just as the alien pulled the rifle out of Travis's grip.

Travis was either good or lucky, or maybe both. The bullet slammed home, hitting the creature in the center of its body, a bulging, unchanging ellipsoid of flesh that apparently contained its vital organs. The thing keened a high-pitched wail loud enough to shatter glass. It released Travis instantly, retracting pseudopods and tentacles. It spun about like a demented top, scattering a foul-smelling goo that pumped out of it like thick, sluggish blood. Then it fell over and lay inert on the ground.

Travis groaned and collapsed as Peter and Chantico rushed to his side. His teeth were clenched in pain. His legs were raw and bleeding where they'd been engulfed by the creature.

"Travis, you okay, man?" Peter asked.

"It burns like the devil," Travis said through gritted teeth.

Chantico tugged at Peter's arm, pointing. There were other forms moving through the blizzard.

"We've got to get away from here," Peter said, "before another one of those things tries to grab us."

"Okay," Travis said, panting in pain. "Just give me a hand."

"Here," Peter said, "Put an arm around my shoulder. Chantico, take his other arm."

The girl understood. She and Peter helped Travis stand. The guide groaned as he put his weight on his legs and his face turned whiter than the snow falling around them. He nodded, gritted his teeth, and they hobbled off.

"Wait a sec!" Peter said. "What about the gun?"

"Leave it," Travis ground out, sweat beading his forehead despite the cold. "No more cartridges."

"Right," Peter said as he and Chantico half carried, half dragged Travis into the forest.

ACROBATS, SINGERS, AND SOLDIERS

The dancing light turned out to be a campfire burning in another forest clearing. Away from the timestorm it was warm and humid, rather like a hot summer night before a cooling rain. There were five gaily painted wagons in the clearing. The oxen that pulled them were hobbled and contentedly munching the sweet meadow grass. Aaron, Travis, and Mundo could see people going to and fro in the light of the campfire. Some women were cooking, some men, mostly stripped to the waist to show off their well-muscled bodies, were juggling or practicing tumbling or acrobatic tricks. A knife-thrower was using a nearby tree as a target while others in the group played musical instruments: stringed lyres and pipes of various kinds.

"What are they, Mundo?" Aaron whispered. "Gypsies?"

Mundo frowned in concentration. After a few moments he shook his head.

"No. They're entertainers of some sort. Their troupe is going to Rome for next week's festival."

"Rome!" Eckels said avidly. "At last, someplace interesting!"

Aaron glanced at him. "You know something about Rome?"

Eckels grinned. "You might say it's an interest of mine." He stepped out from the bushes. "Let me handle this," he said.

"Eckels!" Aaron hissed. He tried to grab him, but it was too late. Eckels strode forward into the clearing. Some members of the troupe noticed him, but they didn't seem alarmed by his sudden appearance.

"It's okay, Aaron," Mundo said. "They seem friendly." He paused. "Of course, it wouldn't hurt to let Eckels find out for sure."

Eckels held out a hand. "*Salve!*" he called.

Everyone looked at him. They were surprised but not frightened as he came from the forest. Aaron felt a little foolish huddling in the bushes, so he also stood. He glanced at Mundo.

"How do we explain you?" he asked.

"Fob me off as a trained ape out of Africa or something. I'll keep my mouth shut until we find out where we stand with these people."

Aaron nodded. "Okay, here we go," and the two stepped out to join Eckels, who was conversing with a balding, bearded man. They looked up as Aaron and Mundo came into the clearing.

"Ah, Aaron," Eckels said expansively, "meet Scipio. He's the master of this delightful band."

Eckels turned to the man and continued the introductions in halting but serviceable Latin. Aaron was impressed. He'd taken some Latin in school, thinking it'd be useful in his paleontological studies, but the only stuff that he could remember were the simple mottoes they used to build vocabulary and learn grammar. Things like "*Vestis virum facit*" ("Clothes make the man"), and "*Manus manum lavat*" ("One hand washes the other"). Somehow he doubted these phrases would be very useful in everyday conversation. He was certainly nowhere as proficient in the ancient language as Eckels appeared to be. Scipio was frowning and listening carefully, but it seemed that Eckels was making himself understood.

Scipio acknowledged Aaron with a civil greeting, but his eyes really lit up when he saw Mundo. He spoke rapidly. Eckels made him slow down a bit and repeat several parts of his speech.

"I'm a little rusty," Eckels said, "and it seems as if pronunciation isn't quite like it's taught, but I'm getting the gist of things."

"What's he saying now?" Aaron asked.

"He's asking about Mundo."

"Mundo's going to lie low and pretend to be just a trained ape until we find out how things stand around here."

"Not a bad idea," Eckels said approvingly. He explained Mundo's fictitious origin to Scipio, who replied, still eyeing Mundo enthusiastically. "He says," Eckels translated, "that he wants to see some of the ape's tricks."

Mundo glanced at Aaron and opened his mouth.

"Uh-uh," Aaron said before he could get any words out. "You're just a trained animal, remember." He made some vague hand gestures. "Do some tricks or something."

Mundo looked at him a moment, then said, "Oooo, oooo," rather unconvincingly. He hopped about a bit, scratching under his arms, then tried to do a backflip, but landed flat on his face.

Scipio pointed and laughed.

"He thinks Mundo did that on purpose. Says it's a pretty funny trick. He wants to know how much we want for him."

"Uh, well, tell him I raised Mundo from a baby and that I couldn't bear to part with him."

Eckels relayed the message and then translated Scipio's answer.

"He says he understands. He's invited us to join them for food and wine."

"That's gr—" Mundo started to say, but Aaron surreptitiously stepped on his foot.

"What have you told him so far?" Aaron asked as they followed Scipio to the blazing campfire in the center of the clearing.

"Very little," Eckles replied. "Just that we got separated from our fellow travelers in a freak storm. They saw something of it through the trees and thought it was very strange."

"Have they seen any of the others?"

"Not so far."

A young man was helping himself to a plate of stew from the cook pot as they approached the campfire. He was about Aaron's age, rather short, and poorly built, with a protuberant stomach and thin legs. He had a bad complexion, light blond hair, and bluish-gray eyes that blinked weakly when he looked up at the newcomers.

"Ah," Scipio said by way of introduction, "Lucius Domitius Ahenobarbus—" He turned to Eckels but fell silent when he saw Eckels staring at the boy.

"Nero," Eckels said in an awe-struck whisper. "Nero . . ."

The things in the snow never approached the huddled forms of Jennifer and Struth. They all disappeared when the timestorm moved off into other dimensions.

The cold also vanished, leaving a blanket of snow six inches deep. The warm summer air returned and the snow began to melt, not too soon for Jennifer. She was frozen through and through, but her first thought was for Struth.

The Mutata lay on the ground like the dead, her heavy-lidded eyes open but apparently unseeing.

"Struth?" Jennifer said hesitantly. She looked around worriedly. Everyone except Klaido had vanished. Klaido looked as bad off as Struth. There was something else lying in a huddle in the dark, but Jennifer couldn't quite make out what it was.

She had heard the very human scream at the height of the storm, quickly followed by the gunshot and she was worried exactly what, or who, that huddled form might be.

She left Struth and approached the dark mass, but backed away quickly. It smelled *bad,* as bad as anything Jennifer had ever smelled, and it looked like nothing she'd ever seen. It decomposed before her eyes. Soon it was nothing more than a pile of jellylike, stinking goo. Jennifer backed away, sickened by its rancid odor and horrible appearance.

She returned to Struth and put her head against the dinosaur's chest. Struth's flesh was cold to the touch. Jennifer held her breath for a long time, waiting, but at last heard the fluttering of Struth's heart.

It sounded weak and intermittent, but at least Struth was still alive.

Jennifer looked up, startled by a sound coming from the woods. It was the tramp of marching feet, the jingling of metal armor and weapons. She looked around, but there was nowhere to run, nowhere to hide. She waited by Struth.

A squad of soldiers marched out of the forest. They carried shields, wore metal breastplates and plumed helmets, and had spears in their hands and short swords sheathed at their sides. Jennifer had seen the movies *Quo Vadis, The Robe,* and *The Last Days of Pompeii.* She knew Roman armor when she saw it.

The soldiers were startled by the remnants of the

snow. Some fell to their knees and scooped up handfuls of the stuff and exclaimed among themselves in what was probably Latin. Then, simultaneously, some of them noticed the rotting dead thing and some of them noticed Jennifer and Struth, and Klaido behind them.

The soldiers who had seen Struth and Klaido leapt to their feet, spears extended, and called out in alarm. One or two of them charged with leveled spears, perhaps showing more bravery than sense because they had no way of knowing that Struth was out of commission.

Jennifer threw herself in front of Struth, her arms extended, and shouted, "No, no!".

The soldiers slowed, approaching more cautiously. One reversed his spear and poked Struth in the hindquarters. Jennifer was half-relieved to see Struth respond with a small moan and a twitch of her leg. Meanwhile, she was wracking her brain to come up with a way to communicate with the soldiers.

"Friend," she said. "Friend."

They looked at her blankly. Speaking Japanese to them certainly wouldn't work. She remembered that Latin was close kin to many other European languages. Unfortunately, she didn't really speak any other European languages, but there are certain words that just about everybody knows. Like the Spanish word for "friend."

"*Amigo,*" Jennifer said, pointing at herself. "*Amigo.*"

The man who seemed to be the squad leader looked at her. He was young and rather handsome. "*Amica?*" he repeated, thoughtfully.

Jennifer nodded. "*Amica, amica.*" She pointed at Struth and then Klaido, repeating that she hoped they were all friends.

The young officer nodded. The men who'd been examining the pile of putrid flesh came up to him and spoke, gesturing with disgust toward the rotting mass. They seemed to be discussing what to do when Struth suddenly groaned and tried to get to her feet.

The soldiers all jumped back, spears leveled, and Jennifer got between them again. She put her arms around Struth's neck and helped her to stand, talking to her in Mutata all the while.

"You're all right," she told Struth. "You've been knocked out by the cold."

Struth's eyes were clouded. Jennifer wasn't sure how much the dinosaur understood.

"These men are friendly . . . so far. I don't think they're going to hurt us."

Struth was weak and groggy, but she also seemed to comprehend more and more of what Jennifer was telling her. The young officer, looking somewhat astonished, asked Jennifer a question which of course she couldn't understand. She imagined that he was surprised that she could talk with Struth. Being unable to communicate with the Romans was frustrating. All she could do was repeat over and over what she hoped was the Latin word for "friend," and smile until her cheeks hurt.

He seemed to get the message, because he nodded and went off to look at Klaido. The Gairk, too, was starting to revive. When he opened his eyes he automatically struck out at the soldiers examining him. Fortunately, Klaido was still sluggish and the soldiers had plenty of time to get out of the way.

"Tell Klaido to take it easy," Jennifer told Struth. "These men could kill him in an instant if they wanted to."

Struth, her head clearing, bobbed her neck in agreement. She spoke to Klaido in the mixture of hoots and grunts that was the dinosaur language and the soldiers were clearly astonished when Klaido answered.

"What did he say?" Jennifer asked.

"He knows we've been captured by the humans," Struth replied, "and is willing to suspend our fight until we can free ourselves."

"Well," Jennifer said. "That's good, I think." She returned her attention to the Roman soldiers. "See," she said, grinning again. "*Amica.* We're all *amica.*"

"How bad is it?" Peter asked Travis as he helped the guide stretch out on the ground with his back braced up against a tree.

"Bad enough," Travis grunted. His face was still white with pain.

"You rest a bit," Peter said. "I'll go find the others."

Chantico was standing by his side. He pantomimed for her to stay with Travis, but she shook her head, indicating that she wanted to go with him. He sighed.

"All right," Peter said. "We can't leave Travis alone. I guess it wouldn't hurt to wait here for a few moments, until the timestorm moves on."

"Go on," Travis said. "I'll be fine."

"Sure," Peter agreed. "You'll be a fine snack for the first bear or dinosaur that comes along. Or whatever crazy animal lives in this timeline."

Peter found a suitable tree and settled down with his back against it. Chantico slipped gracefully to the ground next to him. He put an arm around her and she cuddled close. He didn't realize how tired he was until he stretched out.

"We'll all just rest for a few minutes," he said.

He was tired, he thought, and the thick pad of moss that covered the ground was more comfortable than it appeared. It was pleasantly warm and Chantico was an additional pleasant warmth by his side. He looked down at her. He couldn't see much in the dark night, but she was beautiful. It was wonderful how they were able to communicate without speaking, but he wished they did speak the same language. There was so much he'd like to tell her.

Slowly Peter's eyes closed, slowly his head nodded. He didn't even realize that he was asleep until he jerked awake. He wasn't sure whether the cheeping birds or the rising sun woke him, but he was astonished to see that it was suddenly morning.

Chantico was still sleeping in his arms. He carefully extricated himself and she curled up, mumbling softly in Nahuatl.

He went to check Travis. The guide was sleeping, too, but he tossed and jerked as if he were having bad dreams, and his forehead was beaded with sweat. Peter checked the wounds on his legs. The burn spots had stopped bleeding, but they were red and swollen. Peter hoped they weren't infected. He knew that they had to find medical help for Travis, and fast. Jennifer, he thought, might know what to do.

The guide suddenly awoke. His eyes were bloodshot and looked pained.

"How's it going, Travis?" Peter asked quietly.

It took Travis several attempts before he was able to talk. "Not—not too bad." His voice was dry and hollow sounding. "I could use a drink of water."

Peter looked around. "We should be able to find a stream or something. Maybe first we'd better head back to that building. The others are probably worried about us." Peter looked around, suddenly mystified. The forest looked totally different in the daytime. "Uh—you do know the way back, don't you?"

Travis smiled, but there was pain in it. "Sure," he said. "I think you'll have to give me a hand, though."

Peter looked at Chantico. She, too was awake. She was yawning and stretching like a cat. Somehow, despite the wild flight through time and a night spent sleeping in the woods, she looked fresh and clean. Peter motioned to her.

"Give me a hand with Travis," he said. "We've got to get back to the Floating Stone and find the others."

She took one arm. Peter took the other and Travis got painfully to his feet. Peter saw his eyes narrow with every step and felt the muscles in his arms and shoulders flinch every time his feet hit the ground, but the temporal guide didn't utter a single word of complaint.

It was a good thing Travis was with them, or else Peter would never have found their way back to the clearing. A tree looked like a tree to Peter and he couldn't figure out how Travis could tell the difference between them. He felt a great surge of relief as they stumbled into the small clearing with the stone building.

"Hey, everyone," Peter shouted, "we're back! Aaron! Jennifer! Mundo!"

But no one replied.

"They're gone," he said to Travis.

Travis grunted. "Maybe they're inside."

"Maybe," Peter said, but he was doubtful.

They hobbled across the clearing, helping Travis with every step. There was no sign of the timestorm that had swirled over the clearing the night before, except where Travis had killed the strange creature that had come out of the storm.

The thing had vanished, but it had left its outline imprinted on the ground in dead, withered grass. What was left of the rifle lay in the center of the outline. The wooden stock had been eaten entirely away. The metal barrel was rusted and pitted as if it had been dipped in a highly corrosive acid. Peter glanced at it as they went by, but said nothing. The creature had obviously been poisonous. He hoped that Travis hadn't gotten a dose of the venom.

The stone building had a dozen narrow steps leading to a porch whose roof was held up by four columns. In the daylight they could see that the building had been abandoned for some time. It wasn't a ruin, but the rubble and weeds around it suggested that no one had really taken care of it for a number of years.

"Looks like a temple of some kind," Travis grunted, as they helped him up the stairs. "Maybe Greek or something like that."

Inside, as Peter had feared, it was deserted. There were some stone benches and a battered statue or two that looked Greek to Peter, too, but the rest of their band was nowhere to be seen.

"There's the Floating Stone," Peter said.

He and Chantico helped Travis sit down on one of the benches along the wall and Peter went up to the stone.

"Hey," Peter said, "Aaron left the pieces of temporal mechanism behind. He must have put them down when he tried to deactivate this piece of roadway, and didn't have a chance to pick them up before Klaido came through."

Peter looked at the shiny bits of temporal mechanism. He could use them now. He could take them and go anywhere. Back to Kemet, although that didn't seem like such a good idea. Maybe he could take Chantico home. Maybe they could both go to the Green Town Peter had been to. Peter said that it had changed, and not for the best, but maybe he'd exaggerated. It might be better than this endless trip through alternate realities.

Of course, Peter realized, if he took the mechanism that meant abandoning his friends. He didn't have to take all of the pieces, though. They could go on with their search.

He looked at Travis, who was leaning back on the

bench with his eyes closed. Travis was too weak to stop him. Chantico, who was watching his every move, would come with him. He knew she would.

He got down on his back and worked his way under the stone to get a good grip on the green-glowing hunk of metal that was embedded in its underside. He yanked and felt it shift. He was stronger than Aaron. He could pull it free where Aaron couldn't.

It came loose with his next tug. He slithered out from under the Floating Stone and held it up to show Chantico. He grinned and she smiled back. He looked at the other pieces of temporal mechanism they'd found during their grueling journey among the timelines, sighed, and gathered them all up.

He couldn't do it. He couldn't leave his friends behind. They were all in this together, and they'd all get out together. He had a sudden surge of faith that they would. All working together, all friends again.

"Peter!" Travis said, an edge in his voice.

Peter whirled. Five men stood in the temple's entrance. They carried spears and wore helmets. Two guarded the entrance while three marched forward confidently as Peter dropped the pieces of temporal mechanism behind his back.

He turned to face the approaching soldiers.

"Be careful, Peter," Travis warned.

"Don't worry about me."

One of the three walked slightly ahead of the others. Peter dropped to the floor and threw a sweeping kick that knocked the soldier off his feet. He fell in a heap while Peter wrenched his spear away. Peter wasn't familiar with spears, but he had worked out frequently with a bo staff and a spear is nothing more than a bo staff with a point on one end.

He swung the spear, hitting one of the two standing soldiers smartly on the side of the head. His metal helmet absorbed most of the blow, but it still staggered him. Peter reversed the spear, knocking aside the weapon of the third soldier as he lunged. The soldier staggered forward as his misdirected lunge pulled him off balance and Peter pivoted and smashed a spinning back-kick to his stomach. The soldier collapsed, turning purple in the face as the air rushed out of his lungs.

"Uh, Peter?"

Peter looked up at Travis. The other soldiers were holding their spear points against Travis's chest and stomach.

Peter grounded the butt of his spear and leaned against it, breathing hard from exertion and excitement. They were beaten, and he knew it.

THE GROUP FRAGMENTS

Eckels appeared to be dazed. He kept shooting surreptitious glances at the boy he'd called Nero, whom Scipio had introduced as Lucius something or other. But surely, Aaron thought, Nero was a Roman emperor. If this guy was really Nero, what was he doing hanging out in the middle of nowhere with a troupe of acrobats and actors?

Aaron took Eckels aside and bombarded him with questions.

"You're saying this guy is Nero?" he asked. "Nero, the Roman emperor?"

"Absolutely," Eckels replied.

"But Scipio said his name was Lucius, um—"

"Lucius Domitius Ahenobarbus," Eckels rattled off. "The Romans used three names: the praenomen, which is the personal name given you by your parents, followed by the nomen, which is the clan name, followed by the cognomen, which is the name of the particular family within the clan."

"Right," Aaron said, concentrating. "And none of his names is Nero."

"He took that name when he was adopted by his uncle Claudius, who was then the emperor. Claudius had married Nero's mother, Agrippina, when Nero was a boy. Lucius and Agrippina thought it a, well, goodwill gesture, for Lucius to take a new name—Tiberius Claudius Nero—when Claudius elevated him from stepson to adopted son. Nero was a common name in the house of Claudius."

"You know a lot about this stuff," Aaron commented.

Eckels nodded. He was still watching Lucius, who was trying to get an unenthusiastic Mundo to perform some tricks.

"Oh, yes," Eckels said. "I've always been fascinated with Roman history, particularly the empire. I'm quite an expert on imperial politics and personalities."

"Hmmm," Aaron said. Somehow, he thought to himself, it fit. Aaron didn't know a lot about the Roman emperors, but he knew they were a scheming, often immoral bunch who'd do anything to achieve and then keep power. That included poisoning rivals, even if they were family members. They seemed the sort of crowd Eckels would like to run with. "So, obviously, Claudius hasn't adopted him yet."

"Obviously," Eckels said. He rubbed his chin thoughtfully. "Who knows what's happened in this alien timeline? I'll have to pump Scipio, or Ner—I mean, Lucius—about current history. Maybe Claudius isn't even emperor here. Maybe this timeline has gone off on a totally divergent track."

"Maybe," Aaron said. "Even probably. But be careful. We don't want to raise too many suspicions about ourselves until we figure out where we fit into the picture."

Eckels snorted. "Careful, right. Don't worry, I can handle things."

Aaron nodded. "Uh-huh."

Eckels didn't get a chance to talk with Scipio that night because the troupe master was busy putting his performers through their paces. They were headed for Rome, he'd told them, after years of playing the smaller coastal cities. This was their big chance, their first opportunity at hitting the big time.

Scipio courteously invited the three to spend the night with them and offered to help look for their companions in the morning. Aaron decided to take him up on it. Sleeping in the clearing with the troupe would probably be safer than going it alone in the forest, though Mundo had some doubts.

"You keep an eye on that guy," he whispered quietly to Aaron when no one was looking their way. "I don't like the way he looks at me."

"You're crazy," Aaron said.

"No I'm not," Mundo insisted. "I think he wants to steal me and add me to his show."

Aaron waved his hand dismissively. "Don't worry." He yawned. "Let's just get some rest and we'll find the others in the morning."

"Yeah, well, when I wake up in a cage tomorrow you'll see that I was right."

The next day dawned cool and crisp with a fine, ghostly mist floating in the forest. The mist was gone by the time they finished a cold breakfast, washing it down with goblets of wine diluted with water.

"Scipio says they have to be going soon, but he can spare a few minutes to help look for our friends," Eckels told Aaron.

Aaron ran a hand through his hair. He looked around, perplexed.

"That's great," he said, "but where do we look? I'm totally lost. Mundo, do you know the way back to the other clearing?"

Mundo surreptitiously shook his head.

"Well don't look at me," Eckels said. "I'm not the wilderness guide."

Eckels explained the situation to Scipio and the man nodded.

"He says," Eckels translated, "that he knows the building you mentioned. They passed it yesterday. He'll take us there."

Aaron followed Eckels and Scipio with a mounting sense of trepidation. The two men, deep in conversation, paid no attention to him. Mundo tagged along at Aaron's side, obviously having a problem keeping his mouth shut, but persevering.

Aaron wished he knew what Eckels and Scipio were talking about, but he could only catch a word or two of their conversation. His limited grasp of Latin wasn't enough to make sense of things. Eckels was animated, even eager. Scipio seemed to be a man who liked to talk. Once Eckels got him going he didn't shut up until they found the clearing.

"Here we are," Eckels said, as they approached the structure. "It's a temple, definitely. Hasn't been maintained in recent years." He peered at the inscribed letters chiseled into the eaves of the temple's porch. "Hmmm. It says: 'Dedicated to the Great Mother Isis and the Glorious Emperor, Marcus Antonius.' " Eckels looked at Aaron. "I think we've found the point where this timeline diverges from our history."

"What is it?" Aaron asked.

Eckels looked at him in disgust. "You don't know?"

Aaron shook his head. "I didn't think Marc Antony was ever emperor—"

"You don't think," Eckels sneered. "What *do* they teach kids in school in your day?"

Aaron shrugged as Eckels plowed ahead with his lecture.

"As you know, Julius Caesar was Rome's first emperor." He paused momentarily. "You *do* know that, don't you?"

Aaron nodded.

"All right. He called himself 'dictator,' because the

Romans of his time distrusted kings and emperors, but he was an emperor anyway. He was assassinated in 44 B.C., which set off a civil war that lasted a number of years and saw different factions rise and fall. Augustus Caesar, Julius's adopted son, and Marc Antony, one of Julius's best friends, started out on the same side. The first thing the civil war decided was that the Roman Republic was dead. From now on it would be an empire ruled by an emperor like Julius Caesar. The only thing left to do was choose the emperor. Augustus and Antony ended up fighting for the job. Augustus won. He beat Antony and his Egyptian girlfriend, Cleopatra, at the battle of Actium. So Antony never became emperor in our timeline. He and Cleopatra took their own lives. Augustus became the first Roman emperor in name as well as in fact."

"That's all very interesting," Aaron said. "But we've discovered something else that's important."

"What?" Eckels asked.

Aaron turned in a circle, looking all around the small forest clearing.

"Our friends are gone."

The road was surprisingly well built and was certainly well used. There were companies of marching soldiers, hordes of produce-laden donkey carts and lone travelers ranging from obvious bums dressed in rags to seeming millionaires in gilded litters. And everybody along the road did double-takes when they saw Struth and Klaido.

They marched at the head of the column of soldiers, an uncomfortable Jennifer between them. She knew that Klaido had promised to put aside the challenge that hung between him and Struth until they could figure out their status in this new world, but she found it hard to trust the killer dinosaur.

His habitual expression was a snarl of anger, and an angry-looking Gairk is a terrifying sight. None of the soldiers wanted to be too close to him, and most of the travelers gave him a wide berth, some leaving the road to do so. He and Struth were nonetheless a fascinating sight and provoked numerous stares and comments among the travelers they passed.

Jennifer had no idea where they were going. She couldn't speak the language of their captors and they had no real interest in communicating with her, other than the basic, walk, rest, have a drink—gestured commands necessary to keep the march going in an organized fashion.

She wondered if they were heading for Rome. The idea did excite her. Rome may not have been the first city in the world, but it was among the greatest. In many ways it was the mother city of western civilization and the thought of seeing it in its heyday was exciting. But seeing it as a tourist was one thing; seeing it from the viewpoint of a captive, a virtual slave, was another.

They walked most of the morning with frequent stops for rest and water. The soldiers shared their food with Jennifer, which was tasty, fresh-baked bread. They even offered some to the dinosaurs, but both turned them down.

The procession turned off the main road in the early afternoon, onto a smaller byway that wound off among a series of rolling hills. They passed green pastures with contented-looking cows, cultivated fields being worked by what Jennifer supposed were slaves, and orchards of fruit trees. They finally came to a small settlement isolated among the immense tract of agricultural land.

There was a main residential building and numerous outbuildings among which dozens of people were scurrying on their appointed tasks. Some were carrying bushels of produce, some were setting out laundry on clotheslines, some were undoubtedly trying to appear to be busy so they could avoid real work. It seemed peaceful and quiet, but there was a group of buildings hidden behind the main house and surrounded by a guarded palisade. From this area came the ominous sounds of shouting men and metal clashing on metal. Jennifer wasn't eager to discover what was happening behind the high fence.

Struth and Klaido attracted enormous attention. People stopped to point at them and talk excitedly. Klaido snarled at the gawkers. Struth merely ignored them.

At length a large, fat man dressed in a tunic and toga and accompanied by several armed men came from the main house. He, too, was astonished by the dinosaurs and discussed them animatedly with the officer. Jennifer didn't like his looks. Once he'd probably been handsome, but now his face was dominated by bloated features and a great red nose that indicated he probably drank more than his share of wine. But his looks didn't tell his whole story. There was something else to the man, an almost palpable aura of greed and villainy that instantly told Jennifer she was standing in the presence of real evil.

She had a real bad feeling when he took out a pouch and counted out a handful of silver coins which he handed to the young officer, who smiled, saluted, and waved farewell to Jennifer as he and his men marched away.

The fat man turned to Jennifer and rubbed his fleshy hands together avidly. She knew that she and the dinosaurs had just been sold and she had the sudden realization that she'd better stick with Struth as closely as she could.

The fat man said something in Latin and gestured for her to approach, but she shook her head.

"I'm not going anywhere near you, buster," she said. She turned to Struth and switched to Mutata. "Don't let them separate us."

Struth seemed to grow taller as she stepped forward in an aggressive stance. "I won't," she promised. "I do not like this human."

"I agree," Klaido said, surprisingly. He stepped forward to stand with Struth. "I should eviscerate him immediately."

"No!" Jennifer said. "Wait for our chance. There's too many of them to strike out without a real plan."

Klaido subsided. "Yes," he said. "But someday I will feed on that man's entrails."

Jennifer managed a queasy smile. The fat man had watched the exchange closely, as had his bodyguards. They all seemed relieved when Struth and Klaido backed off from their aggressive stances. Whatever else he was, the fat man was no fool. He seemed to instantly realize that Jennifer could communicate with, and to some extent control, the dinosaurs.

The fat man nodded decisively and spoke again. He gestured for them to follow. Jennifer nodded, but was sure to stay close to Struth as the Roman and his retinue of bodyguards led them around the main house to the walled-in area behind it.

Not only was that part of the estate enclosed by a palisade, Jennifer saw, but there were guard towers at the corners of the enclosure and a squad of four dangerous-looking ruffians was stationed before the main gate.

The fat man, obviously the estate's master, waved imperiously, and the sentinels opened the gate.

Inside the enclosed grounds a large building backed up against the rear wall. It looked like a barracks.

There were some smaller buildings sprinkled around, but the rest of the area was dominated by a large, level field. Men scattered around the field were fighting in pairs. Others were practicing with various weapons, mostly short swords and three-pronged spears. Instructors were harshly encouraging the men to go through their drills or showing them the finer points of combat. A covered grandstand stood in a vantage point where those lounging on it eating snacks and sipping wine could observe the action on the field.

Jennifer suddenly realized that they'd been sold to a gladiator school where men were trained to fight to the death in the arena. No wonder Jennifer had felt the fat man's evil. He dealt in human pain, misery, and death.

Three spectators lounged in the grandstand, a man and two women. Like everyone else they were astounded by the appearance of the dinosaurs. As everyone gradually noticed them, all activity ceased and an eerie silence enveloped the field.

The male spectator came to the edge of the grandstand to get a better view of the newcomers. He was well dressed and wore expensive jewelry, but there was a furtive, ratlike quality to his thin, unattractive features that no amount of gaudy embellishment could disguise. After a moment he beckoned to the fat man. The fat man approached and they spoke quietly, the fat man shaking his head. Finally the rat-faced man dropped him a small pouch. The fat man weighed it judiciously in his palm, then nodded. He shouted at some of the gladiators who'd been training with the three-pronged spears called tridents. Two of them stepped forward and saluted.

"Uh-oh," Jennifer said.

They approached with obvious malicious intent,

their spears gripped in their right hands, thick-woven mesh nets in their left.

They couldn't know the deadly insult they'd thrown at Struth and Klaido. In the culture of the intelligent dinosaurs, they were showing *whiaso,* a right-handed killing, which was only done to unintelligent animals. When the dinosaurs fought equals, they only used their left hands.

Klaido went ballistic at the insult. Jennifer shouted at him, but he paid no attention to her. She was barely able to restrain Struth, who took the insult as well but had less of an all-consuming temper than Klaido, and, actually, was more intelligent as well.

Klaido roared his challenge and thundered forward to meet the spearmen, who were unnerved by Klaido's size and menacing manner. They glanced uncertainly at each other, but held their ground.

One thrust with his spear, striking with a lightning-like jab. It hit Klaido on the fleshy part of his hind leg, but the gladiator hadn't counted on the toughness of Klaido's pebbly hide. The trident's three sharp points barely managed to prick Klaido's flesh.

It further angered the dinosaur. He swung his forelimb, knocking the spear from the gladiator's hand while the other fighter flung his net. He snared the dinosaur—but then couldn't do anything with him. The net tangled around Klaido's forelimb. Klaido twisted his clawed hand more firmly in the strands and pulled, yanking the gladiator right to him. Klaido lowered his head and opened his mighty jaws. The gladiator screamed, but his cry was cut off by the sound of a terrible crunch. Klaido snapped his jaws shut around the man's neck, lifted him off his feet, and shook him like a terrier shakes a rat.

The man died instantly. Klaido dropped him, opening his gaping jaws wide, his daggerlike teeth glistening with the gladiator's lifeblood. He howled his defiance and anger. Jennifer couldn't look at the sickening spectacle. She glanced at the grandstand and saw the three spectators staring at Klaido and his victim with avid, almost lustful eyes.

It was worse to look at the spectators than Klaido's bloody jaws. When Jennifer turned back to Klaido she saw the other gladiator had dropped his net and spear and ran. She couldn't blame him.

Klaido let his other opponent run away. He was content to spurn the body of his victim, raking it with his powerful hind legs until it was an unrecognizable bloody mass. Then to the fascinated delight of the onlookers, he reached down and tore a great hunk of flesh off the dead gladiator, chewed convulsively, and swallowed.

Peter and the others soon discovered that Travis couldn't walk at all, though this didn't bother their captors. They cleaned his wounds, put on a salve that eased his pain a bit, and bandaged him. Then they made a sling with two spears and one of their huge cloaks. At first Travis protested being carried, but it was evident that he could barely hobble while the detachment wanted to move quickly. Four men, one at each end of the two spears, carried Travis along at a crisp pace.

They changed bearers often, Peter taking his turn with the rest. The men didn't seem angry at the extra work. Some of them laughed and joked in a language that Travis declared sounded more like Latin than Greek.

It was, of course, all Greek to Peter, but he'd take Travis's word for it. The soldiers *could* be Roman, of course. Peter had seen a few gladiator movies and these guys seemed to be dressed like Romans. At least like Romans in gladiator movies, anyway. Peter was sure they'd find out sooner or later where they were.

In the meantime, he was worried about the others. Rome—if they were in Rome—was certain to be a big city. Once separated, it would be difficult to get back together again. Of course, they were already separated. Peter couldn't help that, just as he couldn't help being marched away by this squad of soldiers. The thing to do, then, was not worry about it. He worked on not worrying about it as they marched along.

The pace was fast, but the road was easy on their feet and the soldiers stopped for rest at least once every hour. They finally came to a village where their captors took them to an officer who seemed to be the local military commander. It was very annoying. Peter knew they were talking about him, Chantico, and Travis, but there was no way he could communicate with them.

The commander tried out a couple of languages on them, but Peter had to shrug at each one. Chantico tried Egyptian. The soldier frowned as if he almost understood, but eventually shook his head. Peter realized that even if the guy spoke the language used in contemporary Egypt, it still could be a couple of thousand years removed from the language Chantico spoke. It'd be like trying to speak to someone in English when the closest language they knew was . . . well, Latin. She also tried Nahuatl on them, but that really had them scratching their heads.

In any event the commander listened to his underling's story with some interest, issued his orders, and Peter and the others were marched from his office without even an opportunity to say goodbye, if indeed they knew how to say goodbye.

They were taken to the stables where an open-sided cart pulled by a pair of oxen was readied. The officer who'd led the squad that had captured them motioned for them to climb on. He took the front seat. One of his soldiers climbed up next to him to drive. Two more joined Peter and the others in the back as a sort of desultory guard. They weren't very alert. By the time the cart had rolled out of the village they'd taken off their helmets and set their spears aside.

Peter was sure that he could jump off and make a run for it, but even if he'd wanted to desert Travis and Chantico, where would he run to?

He settled back with a sigh and tried to relax. There was nothing he could do but enjoy the pleasant countryside through which they passed, and start Chantico's English lessons.

THE ETERNAL CITY

Aaron spent a long day looking out of the back of the wagon as it rumbled toward Rome. He'd tried some of his Latin on Scipio's performers, but they'd all lost patience with him quickly as he could barely string two or three words together. Eckels spent most of the time on the front seat of another wagon, deep in conversation with the boy he'd said would become emperor.

Aaron didn't like that because he had no way of monitoring what Eckels was saying. He'd told Mundo to keep an ear on the conversation, but that meant that Mundo had to skulk around in the other wagon, pretending to be nothing more than a somewhat intelligent ape. He was able only to report during the infrequent rest breaks. Even then Mundo could only say a few quick words from the corner of his mouth, making Aaron think it was more trouble than it was worth to keep up the fiction that Mundo was a dumb animal.

So far it seemed innocent. Eckels, in his usual careful but efficient manner, was pumping the youth about history and current events. That was well enough. They needed such information if they were going to make head or tails out of their situation. But Mundo reported that Eckels was also, quite unEckels-like, virtually in awe of Lucius. He's complemented Lucius lavishly when he'd cajoled the supposed emperor into singing in a (according to Mundo) thin, reedy, really quite inadequate voice.

The caravan stopped at midday for a brief meal. The wagons pulled off the side of the road in a shady spot. Aaron gratefully accepted the food that one of the performers gave him and he and Mundo sat and ate together, watching the traffic streaming north on the road before them.

Eckels approached when they were almost through and flung himself down on the ground. His eyes were bright, his expression excited.

"Can you believe it?" he asked Aaron.

"What?"

Eckels was in too good a mood to snarl at Aaron's apparent ignorance.

"This is the Appian Way," he said, waving at the road, "one of the great highways leading to Mother Rome herself."

Aaron nodded. "I can't say this whole experience hasn't been fascinating. Still, I'd enjoy it more if I knew we could find the others and eventually get home."

"Eh." Eckels waved off the suggestion of home. He was clearly excited to be here, clearly wrapped up in some personal fantasy. "Home, sure. Someday. But this, this is exhilarating! The power, the might, the grandeur that was Rome!"

"The assassinations, the wars, the bloodshed," Mundo muttered.

Eckels looked at him like he was some kind of insect. "You understand nothing, you monkey. You're not even human."

"Enough of that," Aaron said.

Eckels looked at them both coldly for a moment,

then nodded. "Right. I expect neither of you to understand. You both have limited minds."

Mundo made a face at him and scratched under his armpit.

"Let's not fight," Aaron said playing his customary role of peacemaker. "We have too much at stake. Eckels, why don't you tell us what you learned from Lucius, or Nero. Or whatever you call him."

"Lucius," Eckels said. "For now. He won't be called Nero until he becomes emperor."

"Surely," Aaron said, "this timeline has been so screwed up that that'll never happen."

Eckels shrugged. "Who knows? The lad has royal blood. His grandmother was the daughter of Marcus Antonius and his first wife, Octavia, who was the daughter of Octavius, or Augustus."

"I wish these Romans would stick to one name," Aaron complained. "Antonius became the first Roman emperor in this timeline?"

Eckels nodded. "Correct. Remember that Antonius and Octavius, who in our world became Augustus Caesar, were once comrades. They fought the senators who assassinated Julius Caesar, who was Octavius's adopted father."

"Right. Then they had a falling out and Augustus—or Octavius—defeated Antonius."

"Correct again. Only in this timeline, Antonius won. By that time he'd become, uh, enamored with the Egyptian queen, Cleopatra."

"I saw that movie," Aaron said. "It starred Richard Burton and Elizabeth Taylor."

"Who?" Eckels asked.

"Never mind. Get on with your story."

"I will if you quit interrupting. Anyway, Antonius divorced his first wife and married Cleopatra. They had a son Ptolemeus, named after Cleopatra's royal Egyptian family. Antonius ruled for twenty years. Apparently he was a decent ruler. When he died his son Ptolemeus took over. He was only seventeen when he became emperor, but apparently he was a great and brilliant man. He ruled Rome sixty years and died four years ago at the age of seventy-seven. His reign was a golden age of peace and prosperity. Oh, there were some wars on the periphery of the empire as Ptolemeus extended Rome's boundaries, but they were really minor skirmishes compared to what could have happened. But when he died *his* son, Julius, took the crown."

"I'm guessing that that Julius hasn't worked out as well."

Eckels shrugged. "You'd probably be right. Lucius tells me that he's quite depraved. Bloodthirsty, really. He was forty-five when Ptolemeus finally died. According to Lucius some say that he got tired of waiting and, well, took an active hand in his father's demise."

"He killed his own father?" Aaron asked.

Eckels shrugged again. "Men have done more to become emperor. Anyway, according to Lucius it's one of the rumors." Eckels paused, frowning. "Not that Lucius is the most reliable source. After all, he's probably disappointed with the way things turned out. He has as much of Antonius's blood in his veins as Julius has. If things had turned out differently it could be him on the throne."

"I may not be an expert on Roman history," Aaron said, "but it seems to me that Lucius—as the Emperor Nero—wasn't such a great deal. Didn't he have a lot of people assassinated, including his own mother? Didn't he play the fiddle and sing when half of Rome burned down?"

"It was a lyre, not a fiddle," Eckels said. "And what of it? He was singing an epic poem he'd written, a dirge about the fall of another great city, Troy. It was a eulogy for his city. I never understand why historians made such a big deal about it." Eckels stood. "Looks like we're getting ready to roll again. I'd better get back to Lucius."

"One thing I don't understand," Aaron said. "If this Lucius whatever-his-name-is is royalty, what's he doing with this band of actors?"

Eckels shook his head. "He's obsessed with acting and singing. He was even when he was emperor, you know. Actually, I think he's having something of a holiday while hiding out from Julius. Don't forget that Julius knows Lucius has royal blood. If Julius is only half as ruthless as Lucius says he is, the emperor would have no compunctions about putting him out of the way. Permanently." Eckels looked up at Lucius, who was waving for him to come over. "See you later," he said curtly, and left.

Mundo and Aaron remained sitting under the tree.

"I don't like the way he's acting," Aaron said quietly. "Notice the way he talks about Lucius?"

Mundo nodded.

"There's hero worship in his voice," Aaron said. "You'd better keep an eye on him in case he's planning something."

"Okay," Mundo said in a low voice, and skittered off.

Aaron stood, brushing the seat of the tunic that Scipio had lent him from the troupe's store of clothing. He had the sudden feeling that he was being watched and when he turned he saw that the troupe master's eyes had indeed been on him and Mundo. Scipio nodded at him solemnly as he climbed into the back of his wagon. Aaron nodded back, wondering how much Scipio suspected about Mundo's real nature.

Well, there was nothing Aaron could do about Scipio's suspicions, so he ignored them as best he could while he worried about other things he couldn't control, like the whereabouts of Jennifer and the others.

Since the beginning of this adventure Aaron had slowly evolved into the leader of the group. It was a position he neither sought nor particularly wanted, but it had gradually and emphatically become his and he couldn't evade it. He worried about the others constantly, especially when they were off alone God only knew where.

He sat in the back of the wagon, alone and worrying, as the small caravan trundled down the Appian Way to the great sprawling metropolis, the city of unimaginable splendor and unbelievable squalor, the ancient and eternal city, Rome.

Eckels sat in the front seat of the lead wagon, listening to the boy who in some timelines was the emperor of all Rome tell him about his love for chariot racing. It was one of Lucius's ambitions to be a great charioteer, as well as a prize-winning singer and actor.

It was strange sitting next to the youth. Eckels was, he knew, in the presence of greatness. Lucius—as Nero—was one of the most cunning and powerful men of all time. He had ruled Rome for fourteen years before his untimely and unfortunate demise—and with the right man advising him he could have ruled for another twenty. But he'd had bad advisors and he'd ended up taking his own life in the humble house of a freed slave where he was hiding from the Praetorian Guard. The Praetorians were an elite military unit whose job was to guard the emperor's life, but their shifting loyalties often made—or unmade—the very men they were supposed to watch over.

Truthfully, though, Lucius didn't seem like a great man, at least in this stage of his life. He looked funny with his bad complexion, blinking, watery eyes, thick waist, and skinny arms and legs. He did have a decent voice—and was willing to show it off at the slightest provocation—and he played the lyre, but Eckels soon discovered that he had little liking for the rather monotonous plucking of a couple of strings.

Eckels's clever questioning revealed and discovered that he was more interested in writing poetry and singing and acting and racing chariots than he was in ruling the Empire.

Of course, Eckels realized, that meant that his advisors would have that much more power, that much more leeway when it came to running things. Let Nero sing and mime and race horses as much as he wanted. Someone else could mind the Empire.

He smiled at Lucius who had just finished reciting a stanza from a very long and very boring poem he'd written about the fall of Troy.

"Very nice," Eckels said as sincerely as he could.

"If you think that was something," Lucius said, "wait until you hear the next stanza—"

"Yes, I'm sure it's quite fine," Eckels said before Lucius could launch off on another five hundred lines, "but there's something we should talk about." He glanced around conspiratorially and lowered his voice. "Can you keep a secret, Lucius?"

"Of course," Lucius said. "If I want to."

"You'll want to keep this one. It's very important." Eckels sidled closer and lowered his voice even more. "I'm a magician, you see. A fortune-teller and a seer. Aaron is my apprentice and Mundo is my assistant. He talks, you know, and understands much more than you'd suspect."

Lucius's eyebrows rose. "Truly?"

Eckels nodded.

"I thought there was something strange about that

ape," Lucius said thoughtfully. "But see here, can you prove that you're a seer?"

"Of course," Eckels said, thinking hard. "Let's see. Your mother's name is Agrippina, your father's Cnaeus Domitius Ahenobarbus. He died of dropsy when you were three. His grandfather was Marcus Antonius. Therefore royal blood runs in your veins."

Lucius frowned. "True enough. But you could tell that from my noble bearing. You do know a lot about my past." He looked at Eckels with sudden fear in his eyes. "But that could mean you're an agent of Julius, come to trap me."

Eckels shook his head. He couldn't overplay his hand. "No, I'm not. I'm a stranger here. I've come from a far, foreign land."

Lucius nodded. "Your accent is barbarous and your grammar is often poor. It would be hard to speak so strangely on purpose. All right. Then tell me why you've come. What do you know of my future?"

Be careful, Eckels told himself. You've got him hooked, now don't scare him away. Tell him what he wants to hear.

"Your future is bright and glorious. I see many honors coming your way, many triumphs. You will win uncountable prizes for singing and oratory. You will drive chariots to victory in the Circus Maximus. All Rome will be at your feet."

"They will?" Lucius asked, eyes gleaming. "How will I accomplish all this? How?"

Eckels smiled. He could tell from Lucius's eager expression that he believed. "You will become emperor. And I will tell you how."

The cart with Peter and the others pulled off the side of the road and stopped in a mass of other carts near the city wall. The traffic had gotten heavier and heavier as they neared the city until they parked on the side road jammed with carts carrying wheat and fruits, vegetables, and cages full of chickens, geese, and ducks. The drivers all waited patiently by the side of the road, talking, dozing, or playing a dice game.

"Why're we stopping?" Peter asked.

Travis shook his head. "Looks like they don't allow carts into the city. Only people on foot."

There was a steady flow of foot traffic through a gate leisurely guarded by a squad of soldiers more interested in leaning on their spears than doing any serious work.

The soldiers who had accompanied Peter and the others jumped off the cart, adjusting their helmets, sword belts, and other accouterments. The squad leader motioned for Peter, Travis, and Chantico to get down as well.

"I guess we walk from here on in," Peter said. "How're your legs doing?"

Travis got down gingerly and winced as he put his weight on his legs. "Not too bad," he said. "I'll manage."

The soldiers took it easy on them, setting a pace that was more of a saunter than a march. They stopped at the gate to chat with the other soldiers for a moment. They exchanged greetings and laughs and the sentinels waved them through.

"My gosh," Travis said as they entered the city proper, "will you look at that."

It was more of an astonished statement than a question. There was plenty to look at. Peter had never seen a city more lively or crowded. It was truly amazing.

"Where are we?" Peter asked in an awed voice.

"If I had to guess," Travis said, "I'd say this is Imperial Rome. It has to be. No other ancient city was as big or magnificent or downright jam-packed with people."

The streets, paved with well-worn cobblestones, were twisted and narrow. They were so close together that neighbors in facing buildings could talk to each other from their second- or third-story windows. Peter could see why they didn't allow carts inside the city, at least during the day. There were so many pedestrians crowding the narrow avenues that even only a few carts would have caused massive traffic jams.

The only vehicles, if you could call them that, were litters borne on the shoulders of brawny slaves, two or three to a side. Many of the litters had curtains, but since it was a warm summer afternoon most curtains were lifted and Peter could see their wealthy owners, men and women both, lounging comfortably inside as their slaves carried them through the city.

Many more people chose to travel by foot. Some hurried, intent on their errands, some dawdled to gossip with street-corner idlers or poked about in the stalls that sold fruits and vegetables and household items of every kind.

Knots of pedestrians had gathered on virtually every corner to watch street performers, jugglers, painted clowns, snake charmers with baskets of sleek, lethal reptiles, singers, mimes, sleight-of-hand conjurors, and pavement artists drawing scenes of ship battles or gods or forest landscapes.

The babble of hundreds of voices was amazing. The swirl of activity and color was astounding. The city was vibrant with rich life that Peter had never seen before. The soldiers pushed their way through the mass of pedestrians more or less good-naturedly, exchanging quips and barbs with passersby. The squad leader even dropped a few copper coins into the bowl of a one-legged beggar who was dressed in the carefully patched remnants of a military uniform.

There were more sights than Peter could readily take

in. After passing great apartment buildings a city block in size, colonnaded temples, open marble plazas with fountains and statues, and even an oval open-air stadium that was bigger than any football stadium Peter had ever seen, his mind shut down, refusing to catalog the marvels they passed.

They finally came to an open area set in a parklike region where there were no idlers. They approached a building set back among the trees and green lawns and met sentinels who took their job a bit more seriously than the men at the city walls did.

They stopped at a checkpoint when they were first admitted to the villa. The squad leader accompanied them as two of the sentinels took them to a spacious room devoid of furniture except for a few uncomfortable-looking couches, one of which Travis gratefully sank down upon.

After a few moments two men came into the room. Both were military men. The younger one was obviously an aide to the older. The older man was maybe in his fifties, but he still had a hard-edged look about him. He was fit and trim although Peter noticed that his right hand was maimed. It was heavily scarred and curled into a stiff-looking hook of flesh and bone. Apparently he'd taken a sword stroke that had left the hand virtually useless. Somehow, though, it didn't make him look any softer.

When he spoke his voice was hard, assured, and used to command. He was obviously asking a question, but of course no one could understand him. Peter shook his head. Where was that monkey Mundo when you really needed him?

All Peter could do was shrug helplessly and spread his hands in the universal gesture of ignorance.

The older man chewed his lip and nodded decisively. He said something to the aide who'd accompanied him into the room. The man was a younger version of his boss. He was shorter than Peter, but stockier. He looked in good shape, especially when he discarded the toga that he'd worn wrapped around him like a drape.

He advanced, feet widespread and balanced, arms out, gesturing Peter to come forward.

"I think they want you to wrestle or fight or something," Travis said.

"I guess so." Peter was uncertain. He looked at the older man who nodded once, decisively. "Well, okay," Peter said. He advanced on his opponent.

Chantico cried out a warning or an admonition to be careful, but Peter didn't need anyone to tell him that. His opponent was older and looked as if he knew how to handle himself. But they never heard of karate in ancient Rome.

Peter took a stance facing his opponent sideways, left foot first. The man frowned and came closer as if he wanted to grapple. Peter spun, pivoting backwards on his front foot and caught his opponent above the kidneys with a spinning back kick.

The Roman staggered, and Peter clocked him with an elbow to the side of his head. It landed with an audible *thud,* and his overconfident foe went down like a sack of potatoes.

Peter looked up at the older man. He was looking at Peter with astonishment. He and Peter locked eyes and the older man smiled and nodded. Peter smiled back.

A PROPHECY

The wagon train reached the city walls at sunset and joined the long line waiting to enter Rome. Aaron thought the city was marvelous, bordering on the unbelievable. If it hadn't been for his missing friends, he would've been quite happy spending a leisurely week or two exploring the greatest city of the ancient world.

The only foot traffic on the streets was an occasional procession lit by lines of torch-carrying slaves. During an afternoon rest break Eckels had told him that Rome was dangerous at night. The streets were ruled by thugs who thought nothing of committing murder for the modest amount of loot their victim might be carrying. Only rich men went out at night, accompanied by their household slaves.

Eckels had also told him that all wheeled traffic had been banned from city streets during the day to help keep the streets clear. Now that it was past sunset Scipio's caravan had to compete with the wagons and carts and drays bringing produce into the city. And there were plenty of wagons and carts and drays to compete with.

Eventually they left the mainstream of traffic and sought quieter, but correspondingly narrower and darker side streets that meandered crookedly like cascading mountain streams. Once or twice Aaron thought he saw men lurking in the darkness—the feared thugs who ruled Rome's night—but they never showed themselves or tried to attack the wagon train. Maybe the performers riding shotgun with spears and drawn swords dissuaded them.

At last they came to a residential area set upon the lower slopes of one of Rome's great hills. The wagons stopped before a walled house and Scipio and Lucius went to the gate and spoke to the custodian who welcomed them warmly.

Eckels jumped down from his wagon and strolled over to Aaron.

"Come on," he said. "We've been invited for dinner."

"By who?" Aaron asked.

"Lucius," Eckels said. "He wants us to meet his mother, Agrippina." He looked around. "Where's Mundo? Lucius wants him to come too."

"He's around," Aaron said, jumping to the ground and stretching.

"Mundo!" Eckels shouted. "Get your hairy butt over here!" He looked at Aaron. "This is important, very important. I can't emphasize how important. We've got to impress Agrippina."

"Why?" Aaron asked as Mundo materialized out of the night and silently joined them.

"For one thing, she's connected. She knows all the right people, all the way up to Emperor Julius himself. She's rich and powerful, but she's not sure of her position. That's why she sent her son off with Scipio's troupe. She wanted to get him out of the way for a couple of months while she sucked up to Emperor Julius."

"Did it work?" Aaron asked.

Eckels shrugged. "We'll find out."

Agrippina's house seemed like a cross between a museum and a palace to Aaron. The custodian at the gate led them through wooden double doors into a small vestibule, which opened into a large room called an atrium. The atrium had a hole in its roof that let in fresh air and light. The roof was supported by four gilded wooden columns. A closed cupboard stood in one corner. It looked like a model of a temple. Eckels explained that it was the *lararium,* the shrine where images of the household gods, the family's divine ancestors, were kept. The room was furnished with couches and marble tables. The walls were painted with amazingly detailed forest scenes. Even the floors were decorated by mosaics—an art form in which tiny pieces of differently colored stones were glued together to make a picture. The mosaic on the atrium floor depicted a hunting scene with bowmen, spearmen, and a pack of dogs running down a stag.

The woman waiting to greet them was in her mid-thirties. She might have been beautiful if her face hadn't been so cold and austere.

"Agrippina," Eckels whispered as Lucius went up to her and she coolly presented her right cheek for him to kiss.

Lucius spoke excitedly. Aaron could see Eckels frown in concentration as he tried to keep up with the rapid flow of Latin. If Agrippina was excited by her son's words she gave no sign. She listened, almost coldly impassive to what he had to say, and nodded when he was done.

"What's he talking about?" Aaron asked quietly.

"I can't make it all out. Mostly about his triumphant acting tour. A little bit about us."

Agrippina finally turned her attention to the newcomers. She dismissed Aaron almost instantly. Her gaze lingered a little longer on Eckels. She looked at him closely, as if measuring him. Her eyes widened as she spied Mundo lurking behind Aaron and Eckels and pursed her lips disapprovingly as Lucius prattled on.

She finally cut him off by lifting her hand, then said a few incisive words and strode regally out of the room. Lucius turned to them, grinning.

"What's he saying now?" Aaron asked.

"Well, just that his mother liked us. She's calling a *haruspex*. For now, Lucius says we just wait, have a little bit to eat, then we'll see what the *haruspex* has to say."

Aaron shook his head. "Glad she liked us. I'd hate to see what she'd be like if she didn't."

"Well," Eckels said, "she wasn't too sure about Mundo."

"Hey—" Mundo began, but Aaron stepped on his foot to shut him up.

"Not now," Aaron said, smiling broadly at Lucius. "We'll discuss it later. In private."

Mundo grumbled but said nothing else.

"Anyway," Aaron said, "what's a *haruspex?*"

"A fortune-teller. He tells the future by looking at animal innards—intestines, spleens, livers, what have you."

"Sounds . . . interesting," Aaron said.

Lucius led them deeper into the house where they reclined on couches and ate bread and porridge flavored with vegetables and fish. Lucius was delighted with how Mundo aped the humans by reclining on the dining couches and eating daintily from the plates and drinking honeyed wine from the silver goblets.

Agrippina came into the room just as they were finishing their meal. She was accompanied by two men. The old one was painfully thin and leaned heavily on a long wooden staff. He had a craggy face with deep-set eyes and wild, unkempt eyebrows that looked like a couple of caterpillars glued to the bottom of his forehead.

The other was younger, though his face was lined and what was left of his hair was mostly gray. He had a stiff military posture that his civilian tunic and toga couldn't conceal. He had piercing eyes and a stern expression. He carried his right hand hidden in the folds of his toga. Some moments passed before Aaron caught a glimpse of the hand and realized it was deformed, or perhaps injured, so that its fingers were curved into the shape of a stiff, unmoving hook. Agrippina didn't introduce them.

As she swept into the room she gave Mundo a look that made him scramble off the couch. She spoke in her usual clipped tones, whirled, and strode from the room with the stern-faced man following. The *haruspex* tottered after them.

"She certainly knows how to leave a room," Aaron said.

Lucius also jumped to his feet, threw a few words at Eckels, and followed his mother.

"Come on," Eckels said. "We can't miss this."

"What's up?" Aaron asked.

"The *haruspex* is going to conduct a sacrifice in the peristyle. Then he's going to read the future from the beast's entrails." He looked seriously at Aaron. "Look, you know it's nonsense and I know it's nonsense, but many Romans put a lot of stock in things like this. This could be crucial if we want to enlist Agrippina's help in tracking down Jennifer and the others."

"You're kidding?" Aaron said. He didn't like the sound of that. "Can we do anything to make sure the divination comes out all right?"

"I'll try to think of something," Eckels said, as the three of them hurried out of the dining room after Lucius.

* * *

The peristyle was completely open to the sky. Bigger than any room in the manor, it had been transformed into an ornamental garden complete with a rectangular pool and water fountain, several nice marble sculptures, and shrines to various gods and goddesses placed in hedge-protected alcoves.

The *haruspex* was already at work before one of the shrines as Eckels and the others caught up with him. Lucius, Agrippina, and the military man were watching closely as he held an unlucky chicken upside down by its legs. He ended the rooster's annoyed squawking with a single stroke of his knife, severing the bird's neck. Blood spurted on the marble altar and the chicken's headless body continued to jerk around for a few moments. The seer then made another incision with his scalpel-like blade, reached into the chicken's body, and pulled out a handful of stuff. He dropped the gunk on the altar and leaned over, peering at it closely and mumbling to himself.

Disgusting old faker, Eckels thought. Still, the old man was an impressive sight in the sputtering light cast by the open torches thrust into holders near the altar. Eckels watched him closely to pick up some pointers about the forecasting business.

The *haruspex* mumbled to himself as he probed the chicken's entrails with a bloody finger. Then he stopped, looked closely at the disgusting mess, and pointed dramatically with a stained forefinger.

"Death!" he called. "I see death, clear and hot and near!"

He looked at Agrippina, his eyebrows twitching like tethered caterpillars. Agrippina looked intense and pale. Lucius licked his lips in excitement while the unnamed man looked as stoic as ever.

"Whose death?" Agrippina asked in a low, breathless voice.

The *haruspex* moaned.

"Death," he said, "death, death, death. Bloody and violent!"

Eckels was beginning to realize that fortune tellers weren't exactly specific when telling fortunes. It didn't take much of a prognosticator to predict bloody and violent death in Agrippina's vicinity. After all, in Eckels's timeline she'd murdered her second husband, the emperor Claudius, so her darling son could get the crown. Once ensconced as a power behind her son's throne, she'd had countless others done in until she'd frightened Nero so much he'd had her killed.

She was a hard, clever old witch. Lucius might believe the stories Eckels told him, but he was still a boy, still easily blinded at this stage of his young life. The way Agrippina looked at them with cold malevolence in her eyes showed she was suspicious. Perhaps she thought that they were imperial agents trying to entrap her and her son.

Eckels knew he had to act fast to establish his credentials as a magic man. There was, of course, a simple way to do it.

"Mundo," he said in light, conversational tones, "I take it you've been following what's going on here. Well, you'd better speak up and impress the natives or else I think we're all going to be in deep trouble."

Mundo looked at Aaron, who of course had no clue as to what was happening. Aaron shook his head uselessly.

"Do it, Mundo," Eckels said, smiling sweetly at Agrippina who was still staring at them with cold, empty eyes. "Unless you care to see firsthand what the old lady does to people she doesn't like and has no reason to fear."

That convinced him. Mundo screeched and started hopping around like his tail was on fire. He scared the *haruspex* so much that he almost stuck himself with his sacrificial knife and Agrippina nearly jumped atop the altar to get away from him. The unnamed man put his good hand under the folds of his toga. The significance of this wasn't lost on Eckels. The man was armed, and probably dangerous. Eckels moved so that Aaron was between himself and the man.

And then Mundo started to talk in flawless, perfectly accented Latin.

"Death? Who fears death no matter how bloody, how violent, how near, if it is not one's own? No one here shall die for great deeds are in the future of all." He stuck a furry finger at Lucius, who was watching Mundo's antics with wide-eyed amazement. "All bow to the emperor! All bow to Lucius Domitius Ahenobarbus the Great!"

Mundo fell flat to the ground, prostrating himself, and slapped the marble pavement till the stone rang.

Lucius looked at Eckels. "The ape speaks," he said, delighted.

"Indeed he does!" Eckels said. "And he speaks the truth! He tells no lies and his oracles are clearer than this dodderer's."

Lucius nodded decisively. "Yes, they are." He turned to his mother whose expression was caught somewhere between horror and unspeakable joy. "Eckels says I will be emperor, mother, and his ape confirms it!"

She nodded rapidly, still too stunned to speak. The mystery man's hand reappeared, empty, from underneath his toga. His expression, as always, was unreadable. Or did Eckels detect just a hint of satisfaction gleaming in his cold killer's eyes?

In any event, they seemed to have convinced Agrippina. Eckels smiled. He looked at Aaron, who gaped at him.

"Well," he said, "*that* worked out pretty well, didn't it?"

Jennifer spent the night in a small room in the barracks, surrounded by apprentice killers. Her bed was a pile of dirty straw. When she saw the vermin creeping through it she decided to sleep on the dirt floor, huddled next to Struth.

The cells were too small for one person and two dinosaurs, so Klaido was next door. Their doors were locked, but that was all right with Jennifer. It made her feel safer, as if the locks were keeping unwanted visitors out rather than her and Struth in.

The night was long and difficult. It wasn't only the physical discomfort. It was the cries and moans that came from the neighboring cells. The men in them whimpered like hurt animals and it tore at Jennifer's heart to hear it.

The next day began with the sunrise. One of the trainers went down the line of cells, unlocking them one by one. He looked in curiously at Jennifer and Struth, but hustled quickly by Klaido's cell after unlocking it as the dinosaur glared at him through the grilled window.

The corridor was full of apprentice gladiators. It smelled like a zoo. The men gave Jennifer and Struth a wide berth—and Klaido even wider. They hustled down the corridor after Klaido left his cell. Klaido, bent over because of the low ceiling, nevertheless seemed to puff up with pride.

"The puny things fear me," he said in Gairk, which Struth translated for Jennifer's benefit.

"Who doesn't," Jennifer muttered. They started to follow the gladiators down the corridor, but stopped before one of the cells. Inside, the trainer was shouting at a man who was lying on his filthy straw bed. The man's eyes were only half open. Even from where she stood in the corridor Jennifer could see that he looked flushed and feverish. The trainer kicked him in the ribs, but the man only moaned. Jennifer realized that this was one of the cells from which pitiful cries had come all night. The man was sick or hurt, so weak that even the trainer's blows couldn't rouse him.

The trainer drew back his foot to kick the man again, and Jennifer couldn't keep silent any longer.

"Stop that!" she said.

The man turned and looked at her, a snarl on his face. He started to say something, then stopped as he saw Klaido and Struth looking curiously over Jennifer's shoulder.

He said something that sounded almost contrite, and backed away from the injured gladiator.

Jennifer went into the cell and kneeled next to the injured man. She made a disgusted face. She could smell, among the stink of his unwashed body mixed with the odor of his waste, the vile stench of decay. The man was feverish. He was sweating and shaking as he lay curled up on his side.

Jennifer spoke soothingly and tried to straighten him. He looked at her with uncomprehending eyes, but he was too weak to resist. She pulled his right arm away from his body and he gurgled in pain, too weak to scream.

There was a sword cut on his arm. It was badly infected, oozing pus and other unpleasant body fluids.

"Merciful heavens," Jennifer whispered.

She looked up at the trainer. "Why didn't anyone help this man?"

The trainer shrugged as if he understood Jennifer's words.

"We have to disinfect the wound." She sat back, thinking. She didn't know the Latin word for soap—or even if soap had been invented yet. Considering the ripe body odor that accompanied most Romans, she doubted it. Still, she could flush the wound out with water. And wine. Wine could act as a disinfectant if there was enough alcohol in it. And she needed clean bandages. She had to find the kitchen.

She stood, but the trainer blocked her path with an angry scowl. Jennifer looked him in the eye.

"Struth."

Jennifer stepped back a pace, and Struth moved forward. She reached out a three-clawed hand, and the trainer broke and ran.

Jennifer smiled grimly.

"All right," she said. "Which way to the kitchen?"

The kitchen staff fled when Jennifer and the dinosaurs showed up, but that was all right because it left Jennifer free to assemble her medical kit. Struth looked on interestedly, while Klaido, who was accompanying them because he had nothing else to do, rummaged through the larder looking for something to eat.

Fortunately, the kitchen maids had left the cook fires burning when they ran off screaming at the sight of Klaido and Struth. Jennifer boiled water, sterilizing towels and a sharp knife she'd found. She was rummaging through the storage pots and had just come upon a cask of strong, undiluted wine when the fat man who owned the school cautiously peered into the kitchen, his bodyguards behind him.

Jennifer saw him and beckoned him to enter.

"Ah, there you are," she said. "Come in. *Come in.*"

He looked around cautiously. Struth was standing by Jennifer. Klaido had found a pile of chicken carcasses that were to be the day's food, and was munching contentedly. Jennifer saw the uncertainty on the fat man's face and knew that she had an opportunity that she couldn't pass up.

"We have to get things straight between us," Jennifer said as confidently as she could. "First, I can't keep thinking of you as the fat guy." She pointed at herself. "Jen-ni-fer," she said distinctly. "My name is Jen-ni-fer."

The fat man looked at her and nodded. "Publius," he said, pointing at himself.

"Okay," Jennifer said. "Publius." She pointed at him and he nodded. "Jennifer." She pointed at herself and he nodded again. "Okay. We've got that straight. Now Publius," she said to the bewildered man, "you've got an injured gladiator who needs help or he'll die. It might be too late already, but I'll do my best. I'll need some help. Tell your men to bring along these pots."

She went to the pot of boiling water that had the bandages and knife in it, and mimed lifting it. Then she stepped back, and pointed at Publius, and waited.

It took a moment. Jennifer was sure that Publius knew what she wanted, but he had to decide if he should comply. Finally, he said a curt word to his bodyguard, and one of them sidled into the room, careful to keep clear of Struth and Klaido, who had just finished the chickens and was rummaging through the larder for more to eat.

He lifted the cook pot by its handles, and Jennifer nodded.

"Now follow me," she said, and led the little procession—herself, Struth, Publius, and his bodyguards—back to the barracks.

The injured gladiator looked up with uncaring eyes as they entered.

Jennifer glanced around the cell.

"This place is filthy. It's probably crawling with

germs. Let's get him outside. Now. Pick him up." She gestured to the injured man and was gratified to see that Publius's bodyguards immediately snapped to. Perhaps they were obeying her out of simple curiosity, but at least they were obeying her.

They took the injured man outside and set him down under a sheltered porch. It wasn't the ideal place for medical treatment, but it had to be better than the fetid barracks. Everyone crowded about in a circle, looking on curiously, even Struth. The man looked up at Jennifer with sick eyes.

She took his shoulders and looked down at him. "This is going to hurt," she said. "I wish I could make you understand that it's for your own good."

She held his injured arm out from his body and nodded at one of the bodyguards while pointing at the wine cask.

"Pour the wine over it," she said.

The bodyguard looked at the cask, then Jennifer, then the wine again. He looked at Publius, who shrugged. Then he took the cask and held it to the injured man's lips. The surprised man took a long drink.

Jennifer sighed. "No, that's not quite the idea." She tapped the bodyguard on the shoulder and pointed at the wounded arm.

The bodyguard was puzzled, but shrugged and poured the wine over the open, festering wound.

The gladiator screamed and tried to break free, but Jennifer held him down.

"Okay," she told the bodyguard. "That's enough. Now on my hands."

She cupped her hands and washed them in the wine as the injured man lay back, panting heavily, his eyes the eyes of a trapped animal. Jennifer took the knife she'd sterilized as best she could.

"Now," she told the bodyguard, "the water."

The bodyguard obeyed. The injured man screamed, but soon fell back, unconscious. It was all for the best.

Jennifer carefully began to cut away the man's rotten flesh.

AN APE'S EYE VIEW

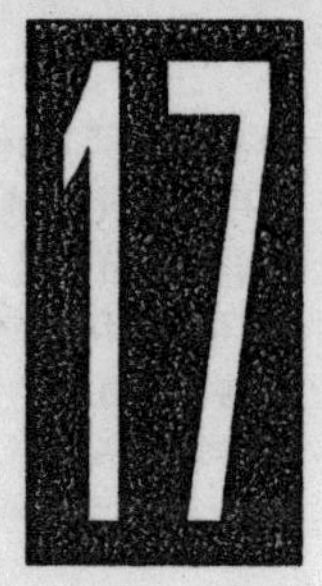

The dark, twisting street gave Mundo the creeps. Sure, a dozen slaves carrying torches accompanied the group heading to yet another dinner party, but the fitful, dancing light cast by the torches was too feeble to do anything but make their surroundings look even more sinister.

They'd been in Rome for three days now, spending the days sightseeing and the nights partying, virtually never out of Lucius's or Agrippina's sight.

Lucius, Mundo had quickly realized, was something of an oddball. Although Eckels had been filling his head with a lot of nonsense about becoming emperor—and he seemed to be listening; who wouldn't?—Lucius was also very serious about his singing and acting. Not that, in Mundo's opinion, he was any good at either, but he was serious about them. He was in great demand around town. People were constantly inviting him to dinner parties where he was expected to perform ("To sing for his supper," as Aaron put it).

Mundo supposed Lucius was so popular because Roman entertainers—singers, actors, charioteers, or gladiators—all came from the lower classes. They could certainly get rich through their particular art and become the toast of the city, but they all started out as slaves, freed slaves, or poor citizens. Lucius was unique. Not only was he a scion of one of the oldest aristocratic families in Rome, he was blood-related to the emperor. You couldn't get much higher class than that. As a result he was a curiosity. Mundo also figured that people thought they were sucking up to Emperor Julius when they invited Lucius to their houses and lavishly praised his singing or oratory.

Mundo, Aaron, and Eckels became part of Lucius's entourage and were expected to chip in with the entertainment, though most of the work fell on Mundo's shoulders.

It was starting to wear a little thin, though Mundo had to admit that he did kind of like the notoriety. While he didn't have much of a singing voice, he felt confident that he could match his oratory with Lucius's any day and come away with the olive wreath. After one performance, in fact, Eckels had told him to tone it down a little and not make Lucius look so bad. It wasn't good for Lucius's reputation or ego to be outtalked by an ape.

They were all so popular on the social scene that for the third night in a row Lucius and the three temporal castaways, accompanied by a dozen torch-bearing slaves, were going to a banquet. This night their host was a man of the senatorial rank who lived on the Palatine Hill. It was an exclusive residential area, but to get there from Agrippina's manor they had to pass the Circus Maximus, which was not in the best neighborhood.

The Circus itself was incredible. It was the largest and one of the most magnificent structures in Rome. A great oval six hundred yards long by two hundred wide, it seated a quarter of a million spectators on its stone and wooden benches. It was used largely for chariot races, but gladiatorial games and other bloodsports also took place within its confines. Lucius had taken them to the Circus just the day before. The chariot races were undeniably exciting. The charioteers were men of great skill and bravery who hurled their animals at breakneck speeds along the oval track to the deafening cheers of the crazed spectators. The gladiatorial combats, however, weren't to Mundo's taste, and he definitely disapproved of the wild animal fights that pitted animals against animals and animals against armed men. The deck was always stacked against the animals.

In the daytime it was a crowded, boisterous, cheerful place, despite the lingering scent of blood and death that clung to it. At night, as they approached from the south, they had to pass vast *insulae,* huge apartment houses three or four stories high that took up entire city blocks.

Mundo looked into the darkness worriedly. He had learned to trust his instincts, and all were telling him to be careful. Rome was a dangerous place at night. There was no police force and gangs of thugs ruled the dark. Mundo plucked at Aaron's sleeve.

"I don't want to sound paranoid," Mundo said, "but I've got a bad feeling."

Aaron looked at him with pursed lips. Aaron hadn't liked it when Mundo had spilled the beans about his sentience. Once they'd talked it over, though, Aaron had realized that Mundo had to follow Eckels's lead. They wanted, after all, to get on Agrippina's good side. She was wealthy and powerful and could help find their friends. She could, but so far hadn't, and Mundo knew that Aaron had been worrying more and more as the days passed.

"I don't think—" Aaron began, but Mundo never learned what Aaron didn't think.

A group of men rushed out of the darkness. They

were dressed in ragged, dirty tunics. They were armed. Some had knives, others had simple but deadly-looking cudgels. There were a dozen of them, as many as in their party, but they were a lot more determined than Lucius's slaves.

The thugs screamed as they dashed forward. The slaves, in unison, turned and ran without even drawing the short swords belted at their waists. Most dropped their torches, leaving only a guttering light to flicker wistfully upon the scene.

Lucius shouted at them to come back and fight, but none listened. They beat it, leaving him and his companions to the not-so-tender mercies of the approaching thugs.

The bullies surrounded them, hefting their weapons, though one of them hung back. He was better dressed than the others. Mundo saw that he wore a toga, which was the badge of Roman citizenship. He was a young man who looked something like a rodent with thin pale hair and protuberant, crooked front teeth. There was no doubt that he was the boss. He said something in a low voice and the thugs advanced.

Mundo looked around desperately. The only weapons between the four of them were Mundo's teeth. It didn't look like good odds.

Lucius stood in the rear of the group and called out in a voice that cracked with fear, "Do you know who I am? I am Lucius Ahenobarbus! I'm related to the emperor himself. By blood!"

That revelation failed to dissuade the thugs. In fact, Mundo caught a glimmer of amusement from their leader's mind. He knew very well who they were. So this wasn't a simple robbery, but a planned beating. Or murder. Mundo scanned the minds of the approaching thugs. Yes. Definitely murder.

There was only one thing to do. He drew himself to

his full height, lifted his arms as menacingly as he could, and let out a high-pitched scream. He charged, his fangs glittering.

As he neared the armed thugs, he had time for only a single thought.

"They're not buying it," Mundo realized, and then there was a loud "*CRACK-A-BOOM*!!!" as the sky erupted over their heads with the loudest burst of thunder that Mundo had ever heard.

It was so unexpected that it startled everyone. It gave Mundo the chance he needed. He hit the circle of thugs at a weak point. He struck right and left with his long, powerful arms and two of the gang went reeling and Mundo burst through.

"Every ape for himself!" he screamed, and then the rain hit, mixed with a howling wind that drove it in cold, stinging sheets. The temperature dropped twenty degrees and Mundo knew that a timestorm, and a bad one at that, was on them.

The landscape flickered crazily and suddenly it wasn't a landscape at all. It was a waterscape. A giant-sized bucket of water scooped out of some alien sea was suspended before Mundo and the others like an unimaginably huge aquarium with clear glass walls.

"Oh, noooo," Mundo mumbled. He skidded to a halt and backpedaled as fast as he could, but it wasn't fast enough.

The forces holding the water hanging before them suddenly crumbled and a liquid wall thirty feet high cascaded down like a relentless waterfall. Mundo floundered desperately, tossed high as the giant fist of water hammered down.

He discovered, to his relief, that he knew how to swim and he poked his head above the surging wave slamming down the narrow, twisting Roman street like a wayward tsunami.

Things bumped into Mundo as he desperately tried to keep his head above water. He didn't care to examine them too closely. He was too busy trying to save his life as the dark skies crashed over his head and the surging water bore him like a piece of bobbing flotsam down the street.

Suddenly he smashed into something big and solid like the side of a building. He rebounded and went under. He gulped a mouthful of salty, vile-tasting water, and tried to choke it out, but more ran into his mouth and lungs.

He desperately grabbed for something, anything, to haul himself out of the water, but his fingers found no purchase. He started to black out and his last coherent thought was, "So this is what death feels like . . ."

Aaron washed up on the steps of a stone staircase, coughing and sputtering. A man ran down the steps and helped him up. He pounded Aaron between the shoulder blades as he tried to clear the salt water from his lungs.

"Thanks," Aaron finally squeezed out when he was able to speak. "Thanks. I'm okay."

The man spoke excitedly in Latin. Aaron strained hopelessly to catch a word, let alone understand what he was saying, but it was no go. He silently damned the communication gap as he smoothed his wet hair back and looked around.

Actually, the flood that had coursed down the narrow street had done some good with the bad. Garbage collection apparently wasn't a priority in the city and the population also had grown far too large for the city's primitive sewage system. The streets had been littered with all kinds of trash, which the flood had scoured away—at least from this immediate area.

Aaron would hate to be where it all got redeposited when the flood ran out of steam.

The flood had also left behind some flotsam of its own. Odd-looking fish, some glowing green with an eerie phosphorescence, flipped and flopped on the damp cobblestone streets. A mass of snakelike things wriggled in a slimy pile as a couple of astonished spectators carefully approached them. Across the street, fetched up against the base of a marble bench was a furry, water-logged mass that looked like a drowned ape.

With a sudden lurch Aaron realized that it *was* a drowned ape—or at least the closest thing possible to one. It was Mundo. He lay quiet and still in a pathetic, soggy pile.

To the astonishment of the man trying to help him, Aaron pulled away and bounded across the street. He ran up to Mundo and turned him on his back. His limbs and neck rolled limply. His eyes were shut and his mouth was open. As Aaron flipped him a stream of water dribbled out of his mouth and down his chin. He wasn't breathing.

"Oh, no," Aaron said. He tilted Mundo's head back and forced his mouth open. More water ran out. He stuck his fingers in Mundo's mouth, pulling his tongue down and cleaning out a vile-smelling, greenish mass of something that looked like seaweed. He pinched the ape's nostrils shut, took a deep breath, and covered Mundo's mouth with his own.

He could hear murmurs of surprise all around him. He dimly realized he'd attracted a crowd, but was too intent on trying to resuscitate Mundo to pay attention to anything else.

He lifted his head, took another breath, and blew again into Mundo's mouth.

"Come on," Aaron muttered as he took another deep breath, "come on."

He breathed into Mundo's still form again, then again and again. He was wondering if he should switch to CPR when he felt a twitch run through Mundo's frame, then a shudder.

"Okay!" Aaron shouted. He gave Mundo another breath of air, then pulled back as the ape grimaced and his eyes snapped open. He looked lost and afraid. His mouth worked frantically then he leaned up on one elbow, turned his head, and threw up a gutful of salt water on Aaron's feet. The crowd surrounding them gasped and drew back. Mundo breathed frantically for a moment then got himself under control.

"You saved my life!" he told Aaron.

Aaron nodded, and looked at his feet. "And this is the thanks I get."

Mundo groaned as he sat up. "Sorry. I was kind of out of it."

"I understand," Aaron said. "It's okay." He looked up. Most of the crowd had dispersed. Seeing a drowned ape on the streets of Rome was interesting. Watching someone bring him back from the dead was entertaining. But then hearing the ape converse with his rescuer was entirely too much. The only one who had remained was the man who'd tried to help Aaron earlier. Aaron gestured at him.

"Who is this guy?" he asked Mundo. "He tried to help me out and I'd like to thank him."

Mundo nodded. "Let me get my breath back." He put his head between his knees and took several deep breaths. At last he nodded and looked up at the man and spoke to him in Latin.

The good Samaritan took this in stride, as if he'd already had his day's quota of surprises and nothing else could startle him. He and Mundo talked for a moment and Mundo nodded and turned to Aaron.

"His name is Cornelius. He's a priest of that temple."

Mundo nodded back over his shoulder. "It's the Temple of Isis."

"Isis?" Aaron frowned. "That's an Egyptian goddess, isn't it?"

Mundo nodded. "I guess so. Anyway, he wants us to come with him and rest a bit. Actually, I think he was really impressed with the resuscitation act that you pulled."

"Want to go with him?" Aaron asked. "I could use a break, myself."

"You could?" Mundo grunted. "I'm the one who was dead for a while."

"Not technically," Aaron said as he helped Mundo to his feet.

"Well, that was as close as I ever want to come."

Cornelius led them across the street and up the steps into his temple. It wasn't as lavish as some that Aaron had seen, but there was a tranquil beauty and simplicity to it that he liked.

"So how did Isis end up in Rome?" Aaron asked.

"I'll ask," Mundo said.

Apparently it was a long story. Mundo and Cornelius talked as the priest led them to a sitting room where he made them comfortable on the reclining couches before running off, he said, to get refreshments.

"Here's the gist of it," Mundo said as Cornelius bustled away. "The Roman people, of course, have their own gods and goddesses, but they're not fanatic about them. They allow others to practice their religion—as long as they don't get too wild about it. Isis, as you said, originally came from Egypt. Her sect in Rome was small and struggling—until Antony became emperor with Cleopatra as his queen."

"Let me guess," Aaron said. "Suddenly everything Egyptian became fashionable."

Mundo nodded. "Correctomundi. Not that Isis worship in and of itself doesn't have a lot to recommend it. Isis, you know, is a mother goddess. Her priests preach love, piety, and gentleness. Not a bad philosophy, really."

"Sounds like Christianity," Aaron said.

"Christianity," Mundo said. "Yeah, Cornelius mentioned that. Small sect, came from the Middle East somewhere. Not especially popular, though he did say that the teachings of its prophet Jesus were so similar to those of Isis that he's been inducted into Isis worship as a saint or something."

"Wow," Aaron said. "That's really incredible. By this time Christianity was fairly well established in my world. It had certainly laid down solid roots by now. So you're telling me that it never got off the ground here?"

Mundo shrugged. "Seems that way."

Aaron let out a deep breath. "Wow. Again. The implications of that are pretty staggering. Do you realize—"

"All right you two," a sudden, stern voice said, cutting Aaron short. "What kind of problems are you causing now?"

Aaron turned to see a tall figure wearing a military tunic with a shining breastplate and a golden helmet topped by a nodding plume. It took Aaron a moment to realize that the Roman was speaking English—and it took him another moment to realize that he recognized the speaker.

"Peter?" Aaron said. "Is that you?"

Peter laughed and took off the helmet.

"In the flesh," he said.

REUNION

"Boy," Peter said, "I sure wish I had a camera. Your expressions were priceless."

Aaron shook his head. "What in the world are you doing in that getup?"

Peter thumped his breastplate. It clanged loudly. "I'm one of the guys. One of the watchamacallits. Pretarians or something."

"Praetorian?" Mundo goggled. "You're one of the Praetorian Guard?"

"Exactly," Peter said.

Mundo looked at Aaron. "They're the emperor's bodyguards."

"How the heck did this happen?" Aaron asked.

"It was the karate," Peter began. He told them how he'd impressed a local military officer who took him to the commander of the guard. "They had me put on a little exhibition," Peter said, "and sort of hired me on the spot." He took off his helmet and showed it to Aaron. "Look at this. Pretty cool, huh?"

"Yeah," Aaron said. "I'm still sort of—"

"Stunned?" Peter asked. "Me, too, at first. But they're not too bad a bunch of guys. They've treated us pretty well."

"Who's with you?" Aaron asked eagerly. "Jennifer?"

"Well . . ." Peter seemed to lose a little of his enthusiasm. "No. I haven't seen her since the night we split up. I was hoping she'd be with you."

Aaron shook his head. "No. Just me and Mundo. And Eckels."

"Chantico and Travis are with me. That leaves Jennifer and the lizards unaccounted for."

Aaron nodded his head gloomily.

"I wouldn't worry too much," Mundo said. "Everyone else is fine. That means they're probably all right, too." He looked at Peter. "Everyone else *is* fine, right?"

"Chantico's just great," Peter said. "And I'm okay. Travis . . . he got hurt a little—but he's getting better."

"Tell me about it," Aaron said.

As they started catching up on recent events Cornelius came in with honeyed wine and some sticky, sugary pastries. They talked and ate and drank the sweet, diluted wine.

"How in the world did you ever find us?" Aaron asked as Peter polished off the last cake.

"Easily enough," Peter said. "I saw the timestorm and figured that you'd be in the middle of it. You always are."

Aaron nodded. "You're right about that. It's got to be all connected with the fact that we're out of time. I wonder if the Mutata are right in a sense? I wonder if our presence in alien timelines causes disruptions wherever we go?"

Peter shrugged. "You got me. Speaking of disruptions, whatever happened to Eckels and this Lucius guy you told me about?"

"You've got me on that," Aaron said. "I didn't have a chance to look around when the wave hit. How about you, Mundo?"

Mundo shook his head. "I have no idea. The water

just picked me up and carried me away. I was too worried about drowning to look for Eckels and Lucius."

"Don't worry," Peter said confidently. "We'll find them. With my contacts and with Mundo to translate, we can find anyone."

"Including Jennifer?" Aaron said wistfully.

"Including Jennifer. Especially if she's still with the lizards."

Aaron nodded, but he wasn't really convinced.

"I wish," he said, "I knew where she was and what she was doing tonight."

Jennifer watched the storm rumble in the distance.

"Dreaming Storm," she said to Struth, which was what the Mutata called the timestorms.

The dinosaur dipped her head and waggled it in a Mutata nod. "It will not touch us, though. We are safe."

Jennifer would have laughed, but she knew that the Mutata possessed no sense of irony.

Safe, she thought. Actually we're lost in an alien timeline, prisoners of a slimy man named Publius Valerius who owns a gladiator school—though she had to admit that so far they'd been well-treated.

It didn't hurt that the man she'd tended not only survived his injury and subsequent infection, he was showing every sign of making a complete recovery. The injured man was grateful, but, more importantly, Publius himself was ecstatic as he saw his profit margin skyrocket since he'd need to purchase much less raw material for his school.

Before Jennifer's arrival, Publius's gladiators were given extremely cursory medical treatment. In fact, most injured men were left to their own devices—basically the healing power of their bodies unaided by drugs or disinfectant. Most injuries inevitably lead to infection and slow, horrible, grueling death since the

Romans had only the most primitive concept of suitable hygiene.

Jennifer changed all that. She taught them as well as she could, given the language barrier. Some of the gladiators thought she was a witch, others thought she was a wise woman, but as soon as it became clear that those who followed her directions recovered more often than not, most were willing to listen to her.

Publius became her enthusiastic supporter. He made every effort to give Jennifer and the dinosaurs exactly what they needed—once he realized their proper needs. At first, for example, he gave both dinosaurs butchered sheep and goats to eat. Klaido relished such fare while it literally turned Struth's stomach. It took a little doing for Jennifer to get across the fact that Struth was a vegetarian, but once she did Publius supplied all kinds of fruits, vegetables, and grain, and Struth was able to pick and choose a palatable diet.

They were allowed the freedom of the fenced-in grounds by day. At night, like the apprentice gladiators, most of whom were apparently slaves or condemned criminals, they were locked in the barracks. Publius had offered Jennifer a place in the manor house, but she prudently decided to stay with Struth rather than test the unknown dangers of bunking under Publius's roof.

Publius allowed no more fights to the death between the dinosaurs and the gladiators in training, though he took a great delight in watching Klaido go against groups of gladiators in more restrained matches. There were no fatalities in these combats, but the first couple of clashes resulted in broken bones and other injuries to Klaido's opponents until Jennifer, through Struth, convinced Klaido to take it easier on his human foes.

Publius was also bemused by Struth's peaceful nature. She was willing to demonstrate her prowess with the spear on targets, but soon became bored with meaningless combat games. Struth didn't regard fighting as recreation. It was a means of protecting one's self or one's group. The concept of fighting for fun or excitement baffled her.

They were safe, Struth had said, and Jennifer guessed that was true enough, though they were cut off from their friends and surrounded by death.

Part of the Roman culture seemed peaceful and serene, part was fascinated with violent death. Jennifer didn't know which aspect of the Roman character was more interested in her and Struth, but given Publius's close association with the dark side of Roman society, she was not optimistic about their eventual fate.

Eckels was as stunned as anyone when the wave hit, but with his great instinct for personal survival he latched onto Lucius before they could be washed apart.

He's my meal ticket, Eckels thought, and I'm not losing my hold on him for anything, tidal wave or not.

It was an intense struggle, but when driven by his sense of self-preservation Eckels was a strong man. Fortunately they got caught by an eddy in the wave and were washed into a side alley where they bounced against a dilapidated tenement building and were left high and dry on a second-story balcony.

"You all right?" Eckels asked Lucius. The Roman nodded groggily, reached down into the folds of his toga, and picked out a wriggling, foot-long fish. The fish stared at him stonily and snapped sharp-toothed jaws within an inch of his nose. Lucius made a disgusted noise and dropped the thing off the side of the balcony.

"You can thank your patron god that you were with me," Eckels said, quick to take credit for their fortuitous escape. "Only my magic saved us from the deluge." Eckels had a sudden inspiration. "Which, incidentally, I called up to protect us from the ruffians."

Lucius looked at him, evidently impressed.

"Your powers are astonishing," he said.

Eckels shrugged deprecatingly and smiled.

"They are in your service, my lord."

Lucius unwound his sodden toga, stripping to the equally sodden tunic that he wore underneath. He looked grim and determined, at least as grim and determined as his adolescent, weak features could look.

"Those weren't common thugs," he said. "Did you notice the man who directed them, who stayed in the shadows?" Eckels nodded. "He tried to conceal his face but I got a glimpse of it. I'd recognize his ratlike features anywhere." Lucius stared angrily at the empty street below.

"He was—" Eckels prompted gently.

"His name is Rufus. He's Julius's confidant and agent, may all the gods damn him. He tried to kill me! Me! To think that he almost deprived the world of my talent!"

"That would be a terrible loss," Eckels murmured sympathetically.

"Yes, it would." Lucius sang a few experimental notes and looked at Eckels in horror. "The soaking has affected my voice. I must get home and change into dry clothes."

Eckels made sympathetic clucking sounds. "By all means. You must be careful to preserve your voice—and yourself to reign as emperor."

Lucius looked at him with a petulant frown. "Do you really think you can make me emperor?"

Eckels nodded. "Definitely."

"How?"

Eckels looked thoughtful. "We will plan a banquet

for Julius," he said. "But first I must visit an apothecary."

Lucius looked at him.

"There are some, hmmm, magical ingredients I must purchase."

A SCHEME IS HATCHED

Aaron and Mundo made it back to Agrippina's house uneventfully, and discovered that Eckels and Lucius had arrived before them. They were in the peristyle, where the head slave was beating the slaves who'd run away from the confrontation with the street gang. It wasn't a pretty sight, though Agrippina looked on avidly. Lucius, to his credit, couldn't watch the brutal scene, and Eckels was vaguely bored with the whole thing, as if something else was on his mind.

Aaron knew that he couldn't stop the administration of Agrippina's severe notion of justice. Nor did he want to watch it.

"I'm going to sleep," he muttered to Mundo.

The ape nodded and accompanied him to the bedroom they shared with Eckels, where the screaming of the slaves could barely be heard.

Aaron tried to sleep, but couldn't, not until the house fell into an uneasy silence but for Mundo's intermittent snoring in the next bed. Even then Aaron tossed and turned. When he finally fell into a troubled sleep, Eckels was absent. When Aaron awoke in the morning, Eckels was still gone.

Mundo was already eating breakfast. Aaron joined him and asked about Eckels.

"I saw him earlier," Mundo said. "He was bustling about. Said he had something important to do. He rousted Lucius out of bed and they left the house right when I got up."

"It must be important," Aaron said, "for Lucius to rise so early."

Mundo nodded and helped himself to another orange from the platter before him. Lucius almost always slept in, because he was usually up late attending dinner parties.

"Wonder what he's up to now?" Aaron said, half to himself.

"Knowing Eckels," Mundo commented, "probably not much of anything good."

"I'm sure we'll find out soon enough," Aaron said. "Anyway—you sure you can find the house where Peter and the others are staying?"

Last night they'd made plans to get together and discuss things. Peter told them that although the Praetorian Guard was headquartered outside the city, he, Chantico, and Travis were actually staying at the manor owned by the guard's commander, a man named Burrus. He told them where it was located on the Averntine Hill, and they'd decided to meet the next day.

"No sweat," Mundo said.

"Then let's go." Aaron looked around, thinking about the night before. "This is a pretty nice looking place—but knowing what goes on behind the scenes gives me the creeps."

The city was as crowded and lively as ever, but in Aaron's mind its image was tarnished by the casual cruelty they'd witnessed the night before. He knew the Romans had slaves. He knew that they enjoyed watching men fight to the death in the arena. But actually being swept up in their preoccupation with violence really brought it home to him.

No society ever devised by man was perfect, but it was suddenly very apparent to Aaron that Rome had a dark side they'd made no attempt to overcome. They catered to their taste for blood and violence in their entertainments and even in the way they conducted their politics. It was deeply disturbing, but Aaron knew that there was nothing he could do about it.

He just had to make sure that this darkness never engulfed him and his friends—and he had to especially watch out for Eckels, who, among them all, would most easily give himself up to the evil that ran wild through the Roman consciousness.

Mundo found Burrus's manor easily. It seemed, though, that getting inside might be another matter, as the entrance was guarded by a pair of Praetorians who took their duty very seriously.

They looked curiously at Mundo and then each other when the ape addressed them in impeccable Latin. Aaron, of course, couldn't follow the conversation, though he did catch Peter's name several times. One of the guards finally nodded and Mundo turned to Aaron.

"Okay," he said. "We're in. This talking-ape business really opens the doors around here."

One of the guards stayed at the entrance, the other accompanied them inside. He left them in the vestibule, which was even more opulent than Agrippina's. The room was bigger, the ornamentation more gaudy if not in better taste. The glint of gold was everywhere. Even the marble statues were gilt in places. After a few moments the guard returned with Peter and Chantico. The Aztec girl was glad to see them, and even greeted them in halting English, though she was glad to talk more volubly in her own tongue with Mundo.

"Where's Travis?" Aaron asked after a moment.

"This way," Peter said, leading them deeper into the magnificent villa. "He's still laid up a little."

"His injuries were that serious?" Aaron asked in concern.

Peter shook his head. "They didn't seem that bad. But they don't want to heal. Don't worry, though. He's pretty tough and he says he's feeling better all the time."

Travis greeted them heartily from his bed and gripped Aaron's hand with his usual strength, but Aaron didn't like his pallor, nor the new pain lines etched in his features. He looked years older than the last time Aaron had seen him.

"It's good to see you again," Travis said heartily. "How've you been getting along?"

"Pretty good," Aaron said, "thanks to Mundo. If he didn't speak the language I don't know what kind of shape we'd be in. We sure can't depend on Eckels."

Travis's face clouded over at the mention of Eckels's name.

"What's *he* been up to?" Travis asked.

Mundo shook his head. "No good, we're sure. He's hatching some kind of plot to put Lucius on the throne."

They explained things, Mundo speaking Nahuatl so Chantico could follow all the details.

"That doesn't sound good," Travis said when they were through.

"I agree," Aaron said. "But other things concern me even more."

Travis nodded. "Like the whereabouts of Jennifer and Struth."

"Let's not forget Klaido," Peter put in.

Travis grimaced. "How could I?"

"Surely we'd have heard," Aaron said thoughtfully, "if they'd turned up in Rome."

"Yeah," Peter said. "You'd think a couple of intelligent dinosaurs would be the talk of the city."

"Unless someone's keeping them under wraps," Travis said.

"But who?" Mundo asked. "And where?"

Travis shrugged.

"If—" Aaron began, and suddenly fell silent. Another man had joined them. He was tall for a Roman, and muscularly built, though he had slipped well into middle age. He looked familiar, but Aaron didn't recognize him until he noticed his damaged hand. Then he knew that he was the man at Agrippina's house the night they'd consulted the *haruspex.* There could be no doubt about it.

He looked silently but expectantly at Peter.

"Oh," Peter said, "that time already." He looked at the others. "This is our host, Burrus. He's the commander of the Praetorian Guard. He likes my karate so much that he took us all in—and now I'm giving him private lessons. Time for one now, in fact. If you'll excuse us?"

"Sure," Aaron mumbled. "Go right ahead. Don't let us stop you."

Burrus looked at him, looked right through him, it seemed. He knew that Burrus recognized him, but the leader of the Praetorians gave no sign of it. He and Peter went off together, leaving Aaron to ponder on the nature of the association between Agrippina and the man who headed the emperor's bodyguards.

Agrippina looked at Eckels with the sour suspicion that was her habitual expression. Eckels had asked for an audience with her and he and Lucius had been granted one in her private chambers.

"You've been filling my son's head with wild ideas," she told Eckels accusatorially before he could even say anything.

"Mother—" Lucius began, but she silenced him with a single withering glance.

Eckels shook his head. "Not at all. Everything I told him was the truth."

"Why should you wish my son to become emperor?"

"Why should you?" Eckels countered.

She pulled at her chin thoughtfully. "It's what he deserves. Also, Julius will certainly move against him if we don't strike first. I think that events have proved this. He fears my son's royal blood. He fears Lucius will take his place."

Eckels nodded judiciously. "Lucius does deserve to be emperor. Just as you deserve to be the mother of an emperor. And I deserve to be the advisor of an emperor."

Agrippina sniffed. "That last part remains to be seen."

"Let me demonstrate," Eckels said. He removed a small glass vial filled with dark powder from his tunic pocket and held it up for Agrippina to see.

She laughed. "Poison? Is that the best you can do? Julius has half a dozen food tasters—"

Eckels shook his head. "Not poison. Watch."

He went across the room and set the vial on the floor. As Agrippina watched he took a candle from his tunic pocket, went to a nearby torch and lit it. He ignited the wick trailing from the vial and stepped back quickly.

The twisted scrap of oil-soaked cloth burned with a sudden surge, running rapidly down to the powder in the vial. The vessel exploded with a sharp bang, startling Agrippina and Lucius as slivers of glass shot through clouds of billowing smoke.

Eckels smiled. Gunpowder. A crude form he'd cobbled together from the inferior raw materials available to him. It had taken him a while to discover a workable mixture, but find one he did.

Agrippina looked at him with a strange expression on her face. She wasn't a fool. She had obviously extrapolated what a much larger measure of this powder could do.

"You *are* a magician!" she exclaimed in a hushed voice.

Eckels smiled modestly. "Let's just say that I'm a man of unusual knowledge. And I want to help your son become emperor."

Agrippina nodded slowly. "Yes. Yes, I really believe that you could."

And she smiled. Lucius smiled. Eckels smiled.

"So . . ." he said.

"You can count on my support." She thought for a moment. "Julius is currently visiting his country estate. My family happens to own a villa nearby. I think we should retire to the country for awhile to get some fresh air. While we're there we should have a banquet."

Eckels nodded. "And invite the emperor."

"Yes," Agrippina said. "My social and political connections will make it imperative for Julius to attend."

"It'll be the social event of the season," Eckels said. He couldn't resist adding, "The emperor will get a big bang out of it."

Agrippina frowned, then she nodded and laughed aloud.

Jennifer was worried.

She hadn't seen Struth since early morning, and then the dinosaur had been more quiet and self-absorbed than usual. Struth usually accompanied Jennifer on her rounds when she tended injured gladiators, but this morning she went off on her own. Jennifer was too busy fixing the usual assortment of cuts, puncture wounds, and broken bones to look for her friend until she finished her medical duties.

It took awhile to track Struth down. The dinosaur was sitting in the sun, wistfully watching a group of children running around playing a game that looked remarkably like the tag Jennifer played when she was their age.

Jennifer sat down in the sun next to her friend. "Are you all right, Struth?" she asked.

"Your human children are as strange as you are, Jhenini," she replied in Mutata. "Who cares for them when they come out of their eggs?"

"Well . . ." Jennifer began, "it doesn't work quite that way for humans. We, um, don't lay eggs. Young develop inside the bodies of human females, and are, um, born. Not hatched."

Struth looked at Jennifer for the first time. "How odd. Some primitive animals on my world produce young the same way."

Jennifer shrugged. "Well, it works for us. Usually."

Struth went back to watching the children romp and roughhouse. "I have to return to my world, soon, Jhenini." She was silent for a moment. "It is time for me to go on a Nesting Walk."

"Oh," Jennifer said.

"If I don't return soon my clutch will be infertile. My hatchlings will never be."

Jennifer put her hand on Struth's neck. Her rough skin was warm from the sun.

"I'm sorry," she said, and her friend gave a blatting sigh of sadness accompanied by the odor of fruit left too long on the vine.

Publius passed by and smiled at them. As usual, he was accompanied by his trusted bodyguards, but there was another man with him as well. This other was clean, well dressed, and heavily bedecked in gaudy jewelry. It took Jennifer a moment to place him. When she saw his rodentlike features she realized that he'd been in the grandstand when she, Struth, and Klaido were first brought to Publius's manor. He was the man who'd paid Publius to match Klaido against the unfortunate apprentice gladiators.

Publius smiled when he saw her and gestured expansively toward her. She smiled as impersonally as she could as the rat-faced man looked her over. He finally nodded and launched into a long discussion with Publius. Jennifer could tell from the fixed look on Publius's face that he wasn't liking what he was hearing.

Publius shot Jennifer a look of mixed pity and resignation that he immediately tried to cover with a smile.

But he didn't fool her. She knew that she was in for something bad—and it was all thanks to the rat-faced man.

A BANQUET FOR THE EMPEROR

Eckels wandered through the gardens of Agrippina's country estate, enjoying the sense of tranquility induced by the warm sunshine, brilliantly colored flower beds, and clean, sweet-smelling air. Rome was fabulous, of course, but he could see where it'd get tiresome after awhile. There were too many people crammed into too small a space making too much noise and garbage. You really needed a place like this to get away from things, to relax and unwind from the hustle and bustle of the big city.

When Lucius became emperor, Eckels decided, he'd get himself a place just like this. He smiled. Maybe this very one. Why not? He liked it. It was conveniently located near Rome. And when he got through with Agrippina *she'd* have no use for it.

He was admiring a particularly spectacular bed of scarlet poppies when a household slave approached. The slave bowed low while Eckels nodded approvingly. His reputation was such that already the slaves feared him and his supposed magic.

And they hadn't really seen anything yet, he told himself.

"My mistress requests your presence in the front sitting room," the slave said.

"What now?" Eckels spoke out loud, irritated.

He was speaking more to himself than the slave, but the slave answered anyway.

"There's a messenger from the emperor," the slave said.

Eckels nodded. Interesting, he thought.

"Very well. Tell your mistress I shall attend her when my meditations are complete."

The slave started to say something, thought better of it, nodded, and ran off.

Eckels grinned. Agrippina really had her slaves jumping. They were afraid of her, but they were even more afraid of a man who dared to keep her waiting.

He strolled around the garden for a few more minutes, then went into the villa. Agrippina was sitting on her thronelike chair in the front sitting room, looking coldly furious. Eckels wondered if the fury was directed at him or the foppishly dressed man standing in front of her throne. Eckels recognized the man, as evidently did Lucius, who was standing half next to, half behind his mother's chair as if trying to hide.

It was Rufus, the emperor's henchman, who had ordered the attack on them a few nights before. He probably knew that Eckels and Lucius recognized him, and obviously he didn't care. Eckels smiled at him blandly. He liked this game.

"They tell me," Rufus said without preamble, "that you're a great magician."

Eckels shrugged. There was no need to overplay his hand. "I have certain talents," he said modestly. "Perhaps you liked the demonstration of power that night on the streets."

There. Now Rufus definitely knew that he'd been recognized. Out of the corner of his eye he could see Agrippina's frown deepen and Lucius become even more frantic with fear.

Rufus nodded. "It was certainly dramatic."

Eckels bowed mockingly. "I strive to entertain."

"Hmmm," Rufus said.

"We've been informed," Agrippina said into the sudden silence, "that Emperor Julius is pleased to accept our invitation to dine, but—"

"But," Lucius said, his fear compelling him to interrupt his mother, "he wants to hold the banquet elsewhere!"

Eckels didn't like the sound of that, but he kept his face expressionless. "Elsewhere?"

Rufus nodded. "Yes. Publius Servius, an old and trusted friend of the emperor's, has a gladiator school in the vicinity. Emperor Julius would be most pleased if the banquet were held at Publius's villa."

"May I ask why?" Eckels said.

Rufus smiled, increasing his resemblance to a rat tenfold. "The emperor has a surprise for you all."

There was another silence. Eckels most definitely didn't like the sound of that, but there was nothing they could do about it. It was clear that Julius was expecting a showdown and he wanted to pick the place where it would happen.

"Well," Eckels said with his best smile, "we wouldn't want to ruin the emperor's surprise."

Rufus shook his head. "No, we wouldn't." He added a few insincere pleasantries, then took his leave.

Lucius immediately started to whine, almost before Rufus was out of earshot. "He knows!"

"Of course he suspects something," Agrippina said in a voice dripping with scorn. "Julius isn't a fool."

Eckels shrugged. "But he can have no idea what's in store for him. What does it matter, here, or at Publius's villa?" His eyes narrowed. "In fact, the villa might even be better. Less of a chance of us getting blamed."

Agrippina nodded, though Lucius looked unconvinced.

"My only question," Eckels said, "is how are we going to make sure that Lucius replaces Julius? There must be others with a claim to the throne."

"There are a few," Agrippina said. "But none of them have the captain of the Praetorian Guard on their side."

Eckels smiled in admiration. During the history of Rome the Praetorians had made more than one emperor. Their support was crucial if anyone wanted to take, and keep, the throne.

"You think of everything," Eckels said.

"Yes," Agrippina said, "I do. Don't forget it."

Eckels smile widened and he nodded, thinking, yes, definitely. She'll have to be the first to go.

Aaron's adventures had taken him to many alien timelines, but he had never met an emperor before. Now that he had, he wasn't too impressed.

He wasn't sure what he was expecting, but Julius wasn't it. He was far too normal-looking, far too ordinary. Given his reputation Aaron had expected someone who exuded a palpable sense of evil, with hard, glaring eyes and features chiseled out of unfeeling stone.

But the Emperor Julius, as it turned out, bore an uncanny resemblance to his seventh-grade English teacher, Mr. Avery. If, of course, he could picture Mr. Avery lolling on a couch while wrapped in a toga. They were both tall, slim-shouldered men with thinning hair and squinting eyes.

Julius reclined alone on his couch. Somewhat disappointingly, there were no beautiful slave girls peeling grapes and feeding them to him one by one. A furtive, harassed-looking man did intercept each tray as it was brought and sampled a bit of each dish before Julius would eat from it, but he was hardly as interesting as a beautiful slave girl.

Aaron nudged Mundo, who seemed subdued and distracted. Aaron figured the ape's mood had darkened because they were attending the banquet as performers, not guests, and he was getting hungry watching Julius and his cronies scarf down everything in sight. Aaron certainly was.

Mundo didn't respond to the nudge, so Aaron elbowed him again.

"Eh? What is it?"

"Who's that guy?" Aaron asked, pointing out the man who stood behind Julius.

"Him?" Mundo asked. "He's the emperor's food taster. He has to check everything for poison before Julius eats it."

Aaron nodded. "No wonder he looks like he has a perpetually upset stomach." He nudged the ape again. "What's the matter, getting hungry?"

"Hungry?" Mundo asked abstractedly. "Yeah."

Aaron looked around the huge *triclinium*, or dining room. It was the biggest room Aaron had ever seen in a Roman house. Apparently Publius, the man who owned the villa, entertained a lot. Aaron had heard that he bought and sold gladiators. He reclined sloppily on the couch next to Julius, obsequious and fawning over the emperor. Aaron disliked him on sight, probably because he knew that the man dealt in human flesh. It wasn't a pleasant occupation and Aaron couldn't believe that anyone who followed it could be a pleasant man.

The couches were all on a raised dais overlooking a central ring where performers from Lucius's old troupe entertained the guests. There were nine couches. Each had a single occupant, though one was empty. Apparently not all of the guests had arrived, but that didn't stop Julius from eating. He didn't believe in waiting.

He occupied the central couch at the front of the room. Publius reclined to his right, a familiar-looking rat-faced man to his left. Mundo had confirmed that he was the man who'd supervised the attack that night in Rome. Mundo said his name was Rufus. It wasn't a good sign that he seemed to be a favorite of the emperor.

Three couches ran down the left side of the room, three down the right. The rows of couches formed three sides of an open-bottomed square, the interior of which was a sunken a stage for the performers. Agrippina, Lucius, and Eckels reclined on the couches against the left wall. Aaron wondered if Eckels's presence among the guests rather than the entertainers was bothering Mundo.

Two of the three couches that ran along the right wall were occupied by a man and a woman Aaron had never seen before. The final couch, the one nearest Julius, was empty.

Aaron was wondering who was late for dinner when he heard the tramp of marching feet and turned to see another familiar face enter the dining room. Aaron recognized him even though his helmet obscured most of his features. You couldn't miss his damaged hand. It was Burrus, the commander of the Praetorian Guard.

Three other soldiers accompanied him, one of whom was Peter. Peter waved surreptitiously as they marched by, then jerked his head backward. Following the soldiers were Chantico and Travis. Travis moved slowly as Chantico helped him along.

Burrus took his place on the empty couch after greeting Julius. Peter and the other Praetorians arrayed themselves behind the emperor, standing in an alert though semirelaxed posture.

Aaron only glanced at them, then turned to Travis and Chantico.

"What are you guys doing here?" he asked, astonished but happy to see them.

Travis grinned. "Peter found out he was going to guard the emperor at the banquet tonight and asked if we could come along. Burrus said sure."

"Burrus did?" Aaron asked.

"Sure."

"Burrus . . ." Aaron said. Suddenly he had a bad feeling about all this. He turned to Mundo, who was crouched by Aaron's side, staring ahead sightlessly.

"Mundo, what the heck is going on?"

Mundo suddenly turned to look at him, his fangs exposed in an angry grimace. "You think because I can read minds a little I know everything? Well, I don't. I don't know what's going on. I don't."

Aaron and Travis looked at each other. Even Chantico, with her limited knowledge of English, could sense that something was very wrong. Aaron started to say something, then thought better of it. Mundo would let them know whatever was eating him in due time. For now, the only thing they could do was stay alert and try to figure out where the trouble would come from.

Although Aaron had the feeling that he knew.

He looked at Eckels, who was drinking deeply from a goblet of wine and sharing a whispered joke with Lucius, who looked stiff-faced and pale. Aaron knew, but there was nothing he could do about it.

The banquet went on. Tumblers tumbled, jugglers juggled, dancers danced. The emperor prevailed upon Lucius to sing a song, but Lucius, Aaron noticed, didn't have his best voice tonight.

And the Romans ate. They ate and ate and ate.

Aaron watched in disgust while Publius, who was packing it away like Julius had announced that all food would be banned tomorrow, summoned a slave with a gold basin. Publius bent over it, vomited extensively, rinsed his mouth out with wine, patted his lips delicately with a napkin, then went back to eating.

No one seemed to think his behavior unusual.

It came Mundo's turn to perform. Aaron led him into the ring by his hand, bowed, and saluted Julius. He gave a short speech in Latin that he'd memorized phonetically, then gestured to Mundo.

Mundo bowed deeply, put on a grave face, then launched into a spirited recital of the famous speech that Julius's grandfather, Marc Antony, had used to arouse Rome against the assassins of Julius Caesar.

He wowed the audience. Even Publius stopped eating and watched Mundo, astonishment bugging out his piggy little eyes. When he'd finished Julius himself offered a salute with a raised wine goblet.

"Never," he said, "have our eyes seen such an astonishing sight. Never have our ears heard such sweet words roll from such uncouth lips. Incredible! To the most wonderful ape we have ever beheld!" He sipped from the goblet that he'd lifted in his toast.

Normally Mundo would have basked in such effusive praise, but Aaron could tell that there was something wrong with him. He looked worried to the point of distraction, but before Aaron could say anything Mundo turned and spoke in a low voice.

"Something's going on," the ape said. "I've been trying to figure it out, but it's too complicated, and there're too many convoluted minds involved."

"You mean Eckels," Aaron said. It wasn't a question.

Mundo nodded. "But more. Agrippina and Burrus are involved. So is Lucius. But Julius and that man Rufus are planning something, too. And that's not all. I've been getting a trace—"

"Friends!" The emperor stood again, effectively ending all conversation. You didn't whisper while the emperor was making a speech. Not if you wanted to live to hear the end of it. "This has been a most wonderful evening. The food has been incredible, the entertainment marvelous. My thanks to sweet Agrippina, for arranging all this, and also to Publius Servius who has outdone himself, as usual, with his fabulous hospitality."

Publius beamed and nodded, suppressing a belch.

"We have seen marvels here tonight, but the night is not over, nor are the marvels." Julius stopped and looked at Rufus, who nodded and gestured to a slave who ran from the dining area. "Tonight," Julius said, excitement growing on his face and in his voice, "we will witness a wonder undreamed of—"

Aaron frowned, wondering what Julius was leading up to. There was a sound behind him of massive feet thudding on marble floors, of claws scraping on stone. He turned.

"A battle between creatures never seen before on this earth."

Struth and Klaido stalked into the sunken pit below the dining area. Struth had a three-pronged spear, Klaido had a pair of massive, spike-studded clubs. Jennifer was with them, looking bewildered and not a little frightened. Behind them, ready if they tried to make a break for it, were a dozen or so heavily-armed gladiators.

"A battle," Julius said with uncontained excitement, "to the death!"

FIGHT AND FLIGHT

21

"Jennifer!" Aaron cried, "what's going on?"

She made an abortive attempt to go to him, but the armed gladiators encircling her and the dinosaurs wouldn't let her through.

"Aaron!"

"Are you okay?" Aaron called out.

"Yes—so far!"

"Hang on. We'll . . . we'll think of something! Mundo," Aaron said desperately, "think of something!"

The ape nodded as Travis and Chantico joined them. They huddled in a tight knot while the other entertainers jostled to see the battle between the reptiles.

"Travis," Aaron said desperately, "what'll we do?"

The guide shook his head. "We're stuck. Somehow we've got to stop the fight, get everyone together, and get out of this place in one piece. But even if we manage all that, then what?"

"Then," Aaron said, "we can leave this timeline! We go back to Kemet, to the Dinosaur World, anywhere."

Travis nodded. "But how do we get back to the temporal roadway?"

Aaron pointed at Scipio and his troupe. "We take one of their wagons—if you think you can find the way back to the clearing where the roadway is."

"I think I can," Travis said. "Once we find the main road, anyway . . . Maybe Jennifer knows how to get to it."

"Okay." Aaron nodded decisively. Things were coming together. Maybe.

There was a sudden noise as Klaido snorted loudly. They had to think fast and move quickly.

"A diversion," Aaron said, shaking a clenched fist in his fevered intensity. "We need a diversion."

"Well," Mundo said quietly, almost diffidently, "there's the bombs Eckels made."

"Bombs?" Aaron and Travis said in unison.

Mundo nodded unhappily. "I knew he was planning something, but he's been keeping it from the surface of his mind. Now, though, he's worrying about when to use them."

"Bombs?" Aaron repeated, flabbergasted.

"Yes," Mundo said. "He wants to assassinate Julius and put Lucius on the throne."

"Good God!" Travis growled.

Aaron frowned grimly. "All right. Here's what we do. Travis, you and Chantico get one of the wagons. I know you're still hurting—"

"Don't worry about it," Travis said curtly.

Aaron nodded. "Okay. Go do it. Expect us in a few minutes if things go right." He paused. "If they don't, you and Chantico had better take off. Every Roman in the world is going to be coming after you."

"What are you going to do?" Travis asked.

Aaron shook his head. "I don't know. I'm making this up as we go along."

Travis nodded. "Luck, then." He turned to Chantico. "Let's go steal us a wagon and some horses," he said.

She smiled at him, having understood maybe one word in ten. But she was tough and brave and determined to help.

Aaron looked at Mundo. "All right. Let's go have a chat with Eckels."

Eckels was surprised to see Jennifer and the dinosaurs come into the ring. He started to consider what effect their presence would have on his plans to blow up Julius.

There was, he decided, no telling. He would have to wait and take his chance when he got it. In the meanwhile, he could enjoy the spectacle of the two dinosaurs fighting to the death.

They didn't need much urging to begin. Klaido knew what they were there for. It looked as if Jennifer tried to talk him out of fighting, but his blood lust was up. Eckels knew that he and Struth had it in for each other and he was betting on the Gairk. Klaido was bigger and stronger and a whole lot meaner than his cousin.

The two lizards jawed at each other for awhile as Struth kept putting herself between Jennifer and Klaido. Klaido made a few rushes at his foe, but Struth was quicker, if not stronger, and she was able to avoid his clumsy thrusts. In fact—

"Hello, Eckels," a familiar voice said.

He turned to see that Aaron had made his way up into the dining area. Mundo was at his side.

"How did you get up here?" Eckels asked, annoyed. "You shouldn't be here—"

"And you should?" Aaron asked. "We came up through the kitchen, if it matters. We have to talk."

"About what?" Eckels asked.

"About the bombs you made."

"Bombs?" Eckels repeated, then, looking at Mundo, sighed. The game was up. That damned monkey had read his mind. "Look," he said, "I'm doing this for everyone. With Lucius as emperor we'll be in position to have anything we want. Power, money—"

"We want to fix the mess you made," Aaron said, "and go home."

Eckels clamped his mouth shut. He knew there was no arguing with the boy. Mundo, though . . .

"How about you?" he asked the ape. "We could run this place. Sure, Nero would be in charge, but we'd be pulling his strings. Think of it—"

"I am," Mundo said. "And I'm with Aaron."

"You . . ." Eckels began through clenched teeth, but he let the word hang heavy and alone in the air. He could force them, overpower them, set one of the bombs off now . . .

Mundo suddenly grinned, showing fangs that could bite through a man's arm with a single chomp of his jaws.

"Don't even think about it," Mundo said. He put a paw out. "Just hand them over."

Klaido had been confined for too long. His pent-up emotions were already at the boiling point. He needed violent action. He wanted to kill and he might as well kill the Mutata and the soft-skinned creature that it treated like a hatchling.

He stalked forward. He already tried a few preliminary rushes, which SStragh had easily avoided, but she'd had made no attempt to strike back.

"You are weak and foolish," he told the Mutata. "I shall crush you with my club and then feast on the body of that disgusting creature of yours." He smiled a savage Gairk smile. "They taste good!"

SStragh trilled a warning. "Jhenini is not part of the challenge that lies between us," she said, waving her spear in Klaido's face.

Klaido didn't bother to reply. He rushed in, clubs held high. SStragh blocked his thrust with her spear. They grunted, pushing at each other. The Mutata was stronger than she looked. For a moment the two creatures swayed back and forth, then a madness exploded in Klaido's brain and he swung with the right-handed club, the one used to kill nonintelligent animals.

The blow was totally against the OColihi, but Klaido didn't care. He was no longer among his kind. None of them would witness his transgression. Besides, SStragh was insane. That much was plain. She was acting like a mindless animal.

The blow caught SStragh on the side of her neck, driving her to the ground. She looked up at Klaido, shock and surprise on her features, blood pouring from a terrible gash in her neck.

Klaido turned to face Jhenini, who was suddenly alone and defenseless.

Peter was shocked, surprised, and dismayed. He watched Struth go down under Klaido's treacherous blow. He watched the Gairk turn to Jennifer, his jaws literally slavering. He watched Klaido raise his club high.

Peter had no time to think. He shouted a wordless scream of challenge, ran past the emperor—who was more than a little startled—and drew his sword. He hurled himself into the air and came plummeting down, sword held above his head.

His aim was good, but he didn't anticipate the force of the blow when he slammed onto Klaido's back. It was like jumping off a building and landing on a saw horse. Peter bit his tongue, choked off a few choice words, but managed to strike Klaido as all the air was driven from his lungs by the force of his landing. He felt his blade bite into Klaido's flesh and heard Klaido roar in anger and pain. He fell off the dinosaur's back, his sword still lodged in Klaido's body.

He hit the ground with another thud and lay there, unable to move or breathe.

Aaron jerked around at Struth's hoot of pain and saw Klaido go after Jennifer. He turned back to Eckels, grabbed him by the front of his tunic, and pulled him off the couch.

"The bomb, Eckels!" he shouted. "Now!"

Eckels reached into the folds of his toga and handed Aaron a metal object the size of a softball. Aaron glanced at it. It was a metal goblet with the top squeezed together. A fuse came out of it. He had no time to examine it closely. He took a step, ignited the oil-soaked twist of cloth in an open torch that was ensconced on the wall, turned, and hurled the bomb into the pit, aiming for the far side, away from Jennifer and the others.

"Duck!" he screamed as loud as he could.

Jennifer saw death approaching in the guise of a grinning dinosaur, but then Peter had come from nowhere and was on Klaido's back, stabbing him with his *gladius.*

The blade bit deep behind Klaido's right forelimb, but then Peter slid off Klaido's back and she heard Aaron's voice scream, "Duck."

She hit the ground.

For a moment nothing happened, except Struth moaned and Klaido roared. He'd dropped his clubs and was trying unsuccessfully to reach the hilt of the blade that protruded from his back.

Then the world blew up.

There was a tremendous explosion that echoed deafeningly off the stone walls that surrounded them. There were odd, whining, ratcheting sounds. Black smoke billowed like a killing fog and Klaido roared again in anger and pain.

The smoke was so thick that it was difficult to see. Jennifer crawled toward Peter, trying to make a wide berth around Klaido, who was still bellowing in the darkness.

She found Peter. He was trying to cough up smoke and breathe at the same time.

"You okay?" she asked.

His mouth worked for a moment, then he managed to suck in a big lungful of air, most of which he immediately coughed out again.

"Okay," he managed to choke. "Breath knocked out. Okay."

Jennifer looked around desperately. Struth still lay on her side.

Eckels's bomb worked. It worked real well.

The Romans panicked. They started to scream and run, even the gladiators, even Julius. Unfortunately, there was nowhere to run to and everyone was partially blinded by the thick clouds of black smoke that billowed from Eckels's bomb.

"What'd you put in that thing?" Aaron yelled above the ringing in his ears.

"Low-grade gunpowder," Eckels yelled back. "And a handful of bronze coins that I'd cut up into little pieces."

Aaron shook his head. He turned to Mundo. "Let's get Jennifer!"

The ape nodded and they started to move off.

"Wait a minute!" Eckels cried. "What about me?"

Aaron looked at him. "Do what you want."

For a moment Eckels looked like a lost soul. He glanced at Lucius, who was stunned and frightened. He tried to look through the billowing smoke at Julius, who was shouting orders to kill them, kill them all. He decided not to wait to see if anyone obeyed the emperor.

"Wait! I'm coming with you!"

He stopped for a moment and looked at Lucius. He shook his head. He'd come close . . . so damn close . . .

Then he turned and ran after Aaron and Mundo, who were trying to fight their way through the panicked Romans.

"Are you all right?" Jennifer asked Struth.

The Mutata bobbed her head. She had an ugly gash in her neck where Klaido's spiked club had torn her flesh. It was bleeding steadily. Jennifer bound it as best as she could with strips torn from her tunic.

Around them was pandemonium. Between the smoke, the screaming Romans, and the angry, bellowing Klaido there was total confusion and chaos.

"We have to get out of here," Jennifer said. "Can you move?"

Struth bobbed her head, but it took her a couple of tries to get unsteadily to her feet.

"Peter!" Jennifer called. "Give me a hand!"

"All right."

He made it to their side and helped guide Struth, who was still wobbly.

"This way out," he said, and suddenly stopped.

Klaido loomed before them. He had abandoned his clubs, but he was still an ugly, ferocious sight. Peter's sword stuck out from behind his right forelimb. Blood flowed steadily down his back and ran down his side. In addition he was bleeding from what looked like twenty or so wounds scattered over his abdomen and face. They were small puncture wounds. Shrapnel of some kind, Jennifer thought, from that bomb.

He was one angry dinosaur, capable of tearing them

to pieces even without weapons. He stepped forward, then a body plummeted from above, landing on the pit's floor. It hit hard and bounced and Publius Valerius looked up, stunned and shaken by the fall.

Klaido looked down. Their eyes met and Publius screamed.

Just for a second.

"Jennifer!" Aaron ran to her as she and Peter guided Struth out of the ring.

"No time," Jennifer panted.

"Klaido's right behind us," Peter added.

"But he's been distracted, for now."

There was the sound of crunching bone and loud chewing behind them.

"Help us with Struth!" Jennifer said.

They guided Struth out of the arena. She was more steady on her feet and soon could walk on her own.

"We'll talk later," Aaron said. "Right now we have a wagon to catch."

"We hope," Mundo added.

RETURN

They were not disappointed. Travis had sent Chantico to the villa's front door where she met the others, then guided them to where Travis had parked the stolen wagon. It was difficult to get everyone, including Struth, loaded, but they managed.

Jennifer gave directions to the main road. Pandemonium still reigned at the villa. The news of Publius's death spread quickly and some of the gladiators were trying to escape from their barracks. No one followed the temporal castaways. Eckels, sitting in the back of the wagon, watched the villa fade into the night. He sighed.

"I could have made an emperor," he said.

"You could have gotten us all killed," Peter retorted. "We should just leave you behind to clean up the mess you made."

"If it wasn't for my bombs," Eckels said, "we'd never have gotten out of there alive!"

"Bombs?" Aaron asked. "How many more do you have?"

"Well . . . just one."

"Mundo?" Aaron asked.

"He's telling the truth," Mundo confirmed.

Eckels made a face at him.

"Hand it over," Aaron said.

Eckels did so with ill grace, then Aaron made his way to the front of the wagon where Travis was driving.

"You doing okay?" he asked.

"Better take over," he said. "I'll navigate."

It was a beautiful night, but somehow Aaron couldn't appreciate it. There was too much on his mind. They'd made it so far, but they weren't exactly making a lot of speed in their overloaded wagon. If the Romans got it together they could easily chase them down.

Aaron worried about it all the way back to the temple, which they had no trouble finding thanks to Travis's sense of direction. They stopped outside to light a few torches from the banked fire pot that Travis had grabbed, along with a handful of spears and swords.

It suddenly began to thunder and the scent of ozone soured the air.

"Timestorm coming," Jennifer said.

"I guess that means we're going to activate the gate," Aaron said. He led the way inside.

"If no one stole our stuff," Peter added.

But the bits of the temporal mechanism were where Peter had stashed them behind the Floating Stone.

"It's all here," Aaron said, as he looked over the lot. He paused. "The only question is, where do we go?"

There was silence for several seconds.

"Don't deluge me with requests," Aaron said. "Chantico, how about you?"

Mundo put the question to her in Nahuatl. She looked at Peter. She seemed to be talking to him as Mundo translated.

"She says that it's all been very strange, all very hard for her. She likes Peter very much. She has never seen another man like him. But she wants to go back to Kemet. That's her home now. She has friends and a high position. She has a good life there. She wants Peter to come with her."

Peter opened his eyes wide, and looked around at his friends.

"I, uh, I . . . jeez . . ." He sighed. "I can't go back to Kemet. I, I need to find my home, too."

Mundo started to translate, but Chantico, with a sad smile, held up her hand and nodded. She went to Peter, stood on tiptoe, and kissed him. "Goodbye, Peter," she said in English.

"Goodbye . . ." Suddenly it became difficult to talk.

Chantico looked at Aaron and he selected the proper piece of mechanism and inserted it into the roadway. He helped Chantico step upon the stone and she had time to wave and say, "Goodbyyyy—" and she was gone.

Peter hung his head and Jennifer put a hand sympathetically on his shoulder as lightning flashed outside. Aaron deactivated the gate leading to Kemet and put the piece of temporal mechanism back among the others. Travis looked at the pieces.

"You know," he said, "we've almost got the entire mechanism here."

"Really?" Aaron said. Tezozomoc, the priest in the Aztec world, had had a prophetic vision and told Aaron that he "would fix that which is broken." The memory of Tezozomoc telling Aaron this gave him a glimmering of an idea. Sudden enthusiasm fired him. "We have to return to the Dinosaur World. I think there just may be a way to fix everything—only we need the time machine to do it."

"How?" Travis asked.

Aaron shook his head. "Let's just go through the gate before the timestorm really hits."

"I don't know," Eckels said. "Remember the reception we got the last time we gated back to the Dinosaur World."

Aaron looked at him. "You can stay here and rot for all I care," he said coldly.

"Aaron's right," Jennifer said. "We've got to move before something weird comes out of the timestorm."

"Why don't we send Struth through first?" Mundo said.

"That's a great idea," Aaron said. "She should be able to defuse any problem on the other side of the gate. How about it, Struth?"

"Yes," the Mutata said. "To be home again. Yes. I shall go first."

There was no mistaking her eagerness to return home.

"Okay," Aaron said. "Let's do it."

He chose the appropriate piece of temporal mechanism and activated the road. Struth clambered up and vanished without looking back.

Winds howled and rain poured down. The roof leaked. Raindrops spattered on the marble floor.

"Who's next?" Aaron said, and froze as terror crashed into the abandoned temple.

It was Klaido.

The creature was panting from exertion and strain. Clotted blood clung to his myriad of shrapnel wounds. Peter's sword was still lodged in his body and the wound still bled sluggishly. His jaws were smeared with blood and scraps of Publius's flesh clung to his dagger-like teeth. He must have followed their scent all the way from the villa. He roared at them and they didn't need Mundo to tell them that he was mad.

"Scatter!" Aaron shouted.

They did, but there wasn't much room to scatter to. They could take the roadway one at a time, but Klaido was sure to get most of them before they could escape.

They were armed with the swords and spears Travis had liberated, but those were pitiful weapons to face Klaido with. Or—

Aaron pulled out Eckels's bomb from his tunic pocket. He lit the fuse with the torch he held, then looked at it as it burned down.

"What are you doing?" Eckels screamed. "Throw it! Throw the damn thing!"

Aaron watched the fuse burn a little longer. He looked at Klaido, who was charging at them, screaming.

"Timing—" he said, and he threw the bomb right into Klaido's open mouth.

The great jaws shut instinctively, swallowed convulsively, and burst apart in a muffled explosion of smoke, flesh, and blood.

"—is everything," Aaron finished.

Klaido toppled forward, his head gone. His hind legs twitched and his forelimbs clawed the air for several moments as blood spurted in a great fountain from the jagged base of his neck.

Peter let out a long breath that he wasn't even aware he was holding.

"Nope," he said. "Good aim accounts for something, too."

Aaron grinned weakly. He felt nauseated, but he knew he'd feel worse in a few moments.

"Okay," he said. "Let's get the heck out of here before something else happens!"

He was closest to the floating stone.

"See you all on the other side!"

He stepped on the stone and vanished.

ABOUT THE AUTHORS

STEPHEN LEIGH is the author of several science fiction novels, including *Crystal Memory*, *Dark Water's Embrace*, and *Speaking Stones*. He is also a contributing author to the *Wild Cards* shared-world anthologies, and has had several pieces of short fiction in such markets as *Analog*, *Asimov's Science Fiction Magazine*, and various anthologies. He is married to Denise Parsley Leigh; they have two children, Megan and Devon. Leigh's other interests include Aikido, juggling, working with his computer, and finding spare bits of free time.

JOHN J. MILLER is the author of more than a half-dozen novels, including *Witchblade: A Terrible Beauty*—based on the popular comic book series—and *The Twilight Zone, Book 1: Shades of Night, Falling*. He has also written a number of short stories, including ten in the *Wild Cards* shared-world series edited by *New York Times* best-selling fantasy author George R.R. Martin. His nonfiction has appeared in magazines as diverse as *Tropical Fish Hobbyist* and *Baseball Digest*. Among his upcoming projects is the novel *Wild Cards: Five Card Draw*, the latest entry in the series, to be published by ibooks, inc. Miller lives in New Mexico.

COMING APRIL 2005

RAY BRADBURY PRESENTS DINOSAUR CONQUEST

by Stephen Leigh

ISBN: 1-4165-0424-9

THE CONCLUDING VOLUME IN A SPECTACULAR SERIES OF TIME-TRAVEL ADVENTURES EVOLVING FROM THE WORK OF RAY BRADBURY!

Aaron Cofield and his friends have traveled to many strange lands as they've watched the timestream fragment before their very eyes. They've met talking dinosaurs, deadly samurai, vicious Conquistadors, and brutal Aztec priests.

Now they must try to repair the flow of history before they are destroyed—either by the timestorms or by their former friends, the Mutata, who blame them for the unraveling of time and have sworn to kill them!

ALSO AVAILABLE

RAY BRADBURY PRESENTS DINOSAUR WORLD

by Stephen Leigh

ISBN: 0-7434-8653-6

BOOK 1 IN THE SPECTACULAR SERIES!

Aaron Cofield and Jennifer Mason are discussing their future when they make an incredible discovery: a newly laid dinosaur egg, ready to hatch! Before long, the two are caught in an astonishing trip across the millennia to Earth's dim past, chased by a psychotic member of a Time Safari.

Racing against time, they face Mesozoic monsters, mysterious time travelers, and a strange new race of intelligent dinosaurs—humanity's allies in their effort to rescue the future!

RAY BRADBURY PRESENTS
DINOSAUR PLANET
by Stephen Leigh
ISBN: 0-7434-8654-4

BOOK 2 IN THE SPECTACULAR SERIES!

The safari to the age of dinosaurs should have been a simple trip, but the hunters soon became the hunted. Now, Eckels, the psychotic time traveler who caused all the trouble, is transported to an alternate prehistoric period by a savage timestorm.

RAY BRADBURY PRESENTS
DINOSAUR SAMURAI
by Stephen Leigh & John J. Miller

ISBN: 0-7434-9302-8

BOOK 3 IN THE SPECTACULAR SERIES!

Eckels, a psychotic time traveler, has shot a dinosaur and meddled with history, destroying the future and trapping himself in the past. Transported to an alternate prehistoric period by a savage timestorm, Aaron Cofield manages to link up with a Travis, a lost Time Safari guide. Together, they must hunt down Eckels and restore the shape of history.

Attacked by sentient dinosaurs, Aaron and Travis escape to an alternate medieval Japan. Caught between dinosaurs, ferocious samurai warriors, and the cold-blooded Eckels, the two must fight for their own survival—and to restore the timestream of our future!